EVEN DOCTORS WEEP

Joanna had been let down in love, and so had
Simon Rivers. They were both doctors, and his
rational plan that they should marry and run
clinics side by side in Tanzania, seemed like the
perfect solution to heartbreak. But what would
happen if Simon found out that Joanna had
fallen in love again—and this time with him?

EVEN DOCTORS
WEEP

BY

ANNE VINTON

MILLS & BOON LIMITED
London . Sydney . Toronto

First published in Great Britain 1967
by Mills & Boon Limited, 15–16 Brook's Mews,
London W1A 1DR

© Anne Vinton 1967

This edition 1980
Australian copyright 1980
Philippine copyright 1980

ISBN 0 263 73457 9

Set in 10 on 10½ pt Plantin

*Made and printed in Great Britain by
Richard Clay (The Chaucer Press) Ltd.,
Bungay, Suffolk*

CHAPTER ONE

IF coming events can be said to cast their shadows before, then this October evening must have provided the exception which only serves to prove the rule. Joanna Temple, or Doctor Temple, to give her her professional title, felt happy and relaxed as she curled her legs under her in the big armchair near the gas-fire in the junior common-room of St Paul's General Hospital, and busied herself with a ballpoint pen and a tablet of writing paper.

She was on call all night, but as there were no D.I.P.s in the hospital at the moment, it was quite likely that she would be able to get some sleep right here in this room. If she was needed she would be bleeped from the main office, and the small receiver in her breast pocket would give out a telling long, long, short, short, short signal, which was her personal S.O.S.

Her pen hovered over the page and wrote, as though inspired, 'November 19th'. She looked the date up in her diary and discovered it was a Saturday and would do very well for her purpose. Of course there was always a risk of fog in November, and Branham wasn't far enough from London to remain uninfluenced by the weather over the metropolis, but she couldn't wait until spring to marry Nicholas: they were too much in love, and he had red hair together with the impatience of temperament which goes with such colouring. Only last night he had murmured into her ear as they said their goodnights in the summer-house down at the bottom of the residents' garden, 'Jo, we can't go on like this. I want to get married.'

So here she was sitting planning her wedding. He wouldn't have to wait for her much longer. She wanted him, too; wanted to give of herself until she was drained of giving; wanted children. Until a few weeks ago her job had seemed paramount in her life; she had worked hard to get where she now was, had never changed her mind since, at the careers conference held in school, she had closeted herself with a woman doctor and asked, 'Please, I want to be a doctor too. Which subjects do I require to take and how much money will I need?'

Doctor Fennemore had genuinely tried to help by providing equal quantities of encouragement and discouragement to the fifteen-year-old girl with the bouncy blonde hair and spaniel-soft brown eyes. She had pointed out that no matter how well qualified one might be at the end of one's schooldays, one's education, medically, was only just beginning. There would be five solid years of study followed by a year as a hospital interne, putting what one had learned into practice.

'If all has gone well you will then be twenty-four, and all your friends in other jobs will be either engaged or married because they will have had time for all the preliminaries. If you are dedicated, however, your job will provide its own satisfaction. You will never be out of work; in fact you will often have too much to do and British-trained medical staff are welcome all over the world. For a woman it's that much harder because she is always having to prove herself in what is still largely a man's world. Some men even say women become defeminised in doctoring.' The woman had smiled. 'Perhaps the profession needs more pretty girls like you to prove them wrong.'

It had not been easy even for someone as single-minded as was Joanna. She obtained the required grades in her school examinations despite the distractions afforded by her younger half-sister, Yvonne. Joanna's widowed mother had married Henry Frear when her daughter was three years old. Yvonne was born a year later and was very like her half-sister in looks, although she had china-blue eyes and a younger child's more helpless and clinging disposition.

When Joanna wanted to go to medical school she found a surprising opposition in her own mother. Tessa Frear objected sharply.

'Where do you think the money's coming from to keep you in idleness for another five years, miss?'

'Well, I thought my father left some money in trust for my education . . .?'

'Education, yes. Surely at eighteen that's over? I think you should get a job and help educate your sister. What makes you think you'll ever become a doctor?'

'Because I've made up my mind and worked hard——'

'You were bottom in history——'

'I don't need history in medicine. I got distinctions in chemistry and biology and a good pass in maths, also Latin . . . I've done everything Doctor Fennemore told me to. Mother, you must——'

Support had come, however, from an unexpected source. Joanna knew all too well that her mother had grown to despise her second husband. He ran a grocery business and was by nature hearty and rather common; Tessa would often remind him that her first husband had been an officer and a gentleman.

'If Jim could see me serving in this shop he'd turn in his grave.'

To which Henry would respond: 'If he's turned as often as you say, Tess, he'll be tied up like a ball of string by now.'

During the row in which Joanna's ambitions seemed likely to be exploded into nothingness, Henry had spoken, and he had said what he had to say in the tones he reserved for special occasions when he brooked no argument.

'If you've got the guts to tackle a job like that, Jo girl, then you shan't want for hard cash. You get yourself in and, by golly, I'll see you're kept there.'

'Stepfather! Do you really mean it?'

'Of course he means it,' Tessa had sneered. 'Suddenly he's a millionaire with money to burn.'

'No, I'm not a millionaire and I have no money to burn. I'm a family grocer with a small bank balance and my fortune laid out in stocks. But I have a young daughter, though I'm nigh on sixty, and if she ever came to me and said, "Dad, I want to be a doctor, or a lawyer or an architect," I would be that proud I'd back her to the limit. I think my Yvonne's too silly and spoilt ever to take the world by storm, but as Jim Temple isn't here to stand behind his own girl and say, "Go ahead, love, with my blessing," then I'll do it for him.' Henry had stuck out his stomach, puffed at his blackened briar and awaited objections which he was prepared to flatten like a tank.

Jo went to the medical school attached to a university hospital and never once looked back in regret. She never missed not having a serious romance; there were many young men prepared to pay court to her beauty, though they shied from her intelligence. One of her tutors fell in love with her, but she could not respond; she was more in love with his subject, which was physical medicine. She qualified just in time to render a final professional service to Henry Frear, who had suffered from angina pectoris for some years and was now in the last painful throes of the disease. She was able to inject the pain-dulling morphine of which he was now receiving the maximum dosage at ever-narrowing intervals, as advised by the family doctor, and after one such injection Henry reached out blindly for the hand of healing.

'Jo, love, you do that real gentle. You've got the proper touch.'

'I'm glad, Stepfather. Let it work now. Try to sleep.'

'Not for a minute, love. I've something to say. I know I'm not going to make it——'

'Oh, come on now: *I'm* not giving you up.'

'I must talk to somebody with sense, Jo. You've got it. You've proved it. Your mother's blind to Yvonne's

8

faults, so I have to tell you. She's nineteen now, and a real looker, as you know. She did just well enough at school to take nursing training and I was glad she was, in a way, following in your footsteps. But she's silly because she's never had any real discipline, and what's happening now isn't really her fault. She thinks she only has to want to take.'

'What's Yvonne up to, Stepfather?'

'She's going around with a married man, a doctor at her hospital. A customer in the shop told me about it.'

'And you can believe the word of a customer?'

'I think so, since she's the doctor's wife and tied down with three small children. Their mutual friends have seen Yvonne with him, and not only at parties, where it might have been innocent, but in lonely lanes in a parked car. Your—your mother won't interfere. She says any woman who's fool enough to allow her husband to stray obviously deserves to lose him.'

'You want me to interfere, Stepfather?'

'If you would, Jo girl. I think I could sleep now, and it isn't the injection, it's peace of mind for the first time in weeks.'

Jo interfered vigorously in her sister's affairs. Yvonne refused, in storms of tears, to stop seeing the doctor in question, so Joanna took her arguments to him direct. She soon discovered that he had no intention of asking his wife for a divorce; he was horrified to learn that his wife knew of his indiscretion. He also said, perhaps rather ungallantly, that it was Yvonne who had originally done all the chasing. His wife was pregnant at the time and he had found Yvonne's interest flattering and relaxing, but good lord, she didn't think he was serious, did she?

Jo made it clear that it was up to him to tell Yvonne that he wasn't serious about her and never would be. He was encouraged to take this step by being reminded that if his relationship with a junior probationer came to light, his job would probably be forfeit.

9

Yvonne, who was not one to suffer in silence, soon let it be known that she was heartbroken and wanted only to die. She never lost her appetite, however, and it was Henry who died, smiling at some secret joke, and it was Jo who saw to the sale of the family business while Mrs and Miss Frear gave themselves up to grief and despair. She did rather well as she got not only one firm of supermarkets interested in buying the shop and freehold site on which it stood but two, bidding against each other. The financial conclusions of this transaction proved to be a great comfort to Tessa, who made plans to rent a small flat in one of the more salubrious London suburbs and take her atrophied social life out of mothballs. Yvonne would have been quite content to surrender her career and live a butterfly existence, but Tessa put her foot down for once.

'You wanted to be a nurse and you'll finish your training. Your father worked hard in his business and now I'm better off than ever he was in his lifetime. I'm not going to have you draining Henry's substance away. When you're twenty-one you'll get your share. That's the way he willed things. Joanna, of course, has been helped and doesn't expect anything, do you, dear?'

'No, of course not, Mother.'

Since her elder daughter had qualified, Tessa regarded her with considerable respect. She never missed an opportunity of telling the most casual of acquaintances of her offspring's status and prospects. 'After her compulsory year in hospital she worked for her M.D. diploma and they asked her to stay on. That girl is so single-minded, she'll do wonders.'

A still mournful Yvonne, suffering the double humiliation of both being rejected in love and having her friends at the hospital acquainted of it, wanted to get away from the nudges, the pointing fingers.

'Transfer to St Paul's and we'll be together,' Joanna advised sympathetically. 'I know you're hurt, Yvonne, but it was never any good falling for that man. He would never have risked his job for you. He merely wanted to have his cake and eat it. St Paul's is bigger than your hospital and there are lots of unattached young men, a whole medical school of them. You're so pretty you're bound to be in demand. Even I have a good time, and I'm an old sobersides compared with my little sister.'

'You're still quite pretty, though, Jo,' assured the other, as one aware of her own physical perfections.

Joanna smiled and said, 'Well, thank you! I shall apply for my old-age pension next week, after a sisterly crack like that. Would you like me to speak to the P.N.O.?'

'Yes, do.' Even for a change of location Yvonne Frear depended on other people to act for her.

It was now a year since Yvonne had joined her sister at St Paul's, and she appeared to have settled down very well. After the first few weeks she had ceased to seek her half-sister's company, though occasionally Joanna saw her on the wards looking her usual blithe self, or in the town with various young men apparently hanging on to her every word. She was obviously having a good time socially, though one of the two sister tutors did once complain to Joanna that Nurse Frear was inclined to skip lectures and scrape through examinations by the skin of her teeth.

'She'll probably marry and retire from the fray of hospital life, anyway,' Joanna mused to herself. Her hope was that Yvonne did just this without bringing any more sorrow to either herself or another. Sometimes physical beauty can be a burden; with it should go the responsibility of a beautiful mind which can handle difficult situations.

As she curled in front of the gas-fire, planning her own surrender to the pleasures of love, she remembered a conversation she had had with Yvonne only a few days previously.

'Jo, I'm in love.'

'Oh, dear! Is this the ninety-ninth or the hundredth time, Yvonne?'

'No, seriously, I do really like him. There's just one snag. He's engaged to somebody else, sort of unofficially.'

'Oh? How do you mean, unofficially?'

'Well, there's no engagement ring, they have a sort of understanding. But he likes me too, and I know you'll say I've smashed things up unless I explain the situation to you. Do you blame me for seeing him in the circumstances?'

'Does the other girl know he's seeing you?'

'I don't know. But every time we do meet it gets a little more serious. He's going to have to decide one way or the other.'

'Exactly. I think you should put the ball in his court and make it clear he can't have two strings to his bow. But if he decides against you, Yvonne, take it right on the chin. Don't go to pieces like you did before.'

'You can't have much faith in me, big sister, if you think I wouldn't be sure of myself a second time. I'm going to tell him next Friday that I won't see him any more unless he makes up his mind once and for all that it's me he wants. And I know now which way he'll swing. You mustn't think I'm a fool.'

'No. I can't help feeling sorry for the other girl, though. Still, you can't be one hundred per cent sure of any man until you're actually married to him. That's the way they are.'

I should talk, she had thought wryly, *I'm* not actually engaged to Nicky. Only I'm the odd one who is absolutely sure of her man. We don't need rings to seal our bargains.

'Aren't you going to tell me who he is?' she had pressed. 'I'm terribly curious.'

'No, I'm not. When I have his ring on my finger I'll flaunt it, and him, around. You can't blame me for not confiding more at the moment. Being you, you'd discover some snag. I don't know her name either, but I hate her on principle. Now I must go. I'm still a working girl, unfortunately.'

This was Friday evening and Yvonne would be out somewhere with her young man, persuading him to lay his cards on the table regarding her.

I can't help hoping, if he's steady and successful, that she deserves and wins him, Joanna thought fondly. The other girl should have hung on tight if she really cared. Obviously she's been slipping lately. Maybe she has been too busy to keep herself looking attractive, and it simply doesn't pay.

She wrote on her note-pad: 'Who are we inviting to the wedding? Is it to be a big affair, in church, or quietly at the registrar's? I want to continue working afterwards. Is that O.K. with you, darling?'

Her eyes glazed into a dream and she could easily have slid into sleep, but she forced herself to get up and turn off the gas-fire. The room was over-heated and it was barely ten o'clock; too early to settle down and really relax.

Bill Whitley, the ear, nose and throat house-surgeon, burst into the room like a bomb.

'Hello, Jo: you on call?'

'Yes. But all seems to be quiet on the Western Front.'

'Don't count on it. I have a feeling about this coming night and my mother was extremely psychic. I think it's going to be a stinker. I'm on call too, and I've just been taking a dekko at my five tonsillectomies. If none doesn't haemorrhage before morning I'll eat my stethoscope. They're all extremely restless. One starts the others off and just anything can happen. Since we lost that kiddy in the spring, I've been extremely nervous.'

'Well, my hunch is that it's going to be a quiet night,' Joanna said firmly, 'and I'll bet I'm just as psychic as your mother. All your tonsillectomies will go to sleep and be shouting for their cornflakes in the morning, you'll see.'

At that moment the receiver in her pocket began to buzz and then bleeped clearly; long, long, short, short, short.

'That's me,' she smiled, going over to the wall telephone, 'but I'm sure it's just routine. Doctor Temple here,' she announced herself into the mouthpiece. 'It's Mrs Mayhew, on my ward,' she told the E.N.T. junior. 'She can't sleep and she wants to see me. She's keeping the ward awake, the night-senior says. I'd better go along and calm her down. See you in a few minutes for a nice fresh cup of coffee.'

Joanna always liked the look of the hospital at night. The corridors were dim and quiet and the wards she passed were closed, with only the red-shaded light hanging low over the staff table, where the senior night nurse did her paper work and kept the patients' notes; the red light always made Jo think of Christmas. She didn't hurry because it wasn't as if Mrs Mayhew was an emergency, and of course she couldn't help thinking of Nicholas and wondering if the surgical lecture he was attending at the University was interesting or dull as ditchwater.

He had said, 'If I am going to get married I must better my degree and do some studying. I'll need a better job, more money . . .'

Jo gave a little skip of sheer happiness outside the deserted, dark ophthalmic clinic. Here were the surgical wards in a sort of semi-circle, equidistant from the major and minor theatres. All this was modern, expertly planned and entirely functional; there were Nick's gynae wards: he used to make a joke about being the only house-surgeon with one ward to bother about. 'Men,' he would add, 'do not have gynaecological complaints. I have it here, lads,' and he would point knowingly to his blazing red head. Nowadays he couldn't boast, however, for Sir Philip Carney, his consultant, had been given a second ward due to pressure of work. It would appear that twice the number of women had gynaecological troubles compared with those who had other complaints.

The medical and geriatric wards were in the old part

of the building, what had once been the whole of St Paul's General Hospital when Branham was a small market town. Now it was a London dormitory with large numbers of commuter families for which it had provided blocks of flats and garden estates. Its hospital had pushed outwards and upwards and now had its own medical school. Students who failed to get in at London University were glad to be accepted by Branham: the bright lights of the metropolis were only twenty miles distant and the North-Eastern line provided a regular service of trains.

Joanna had to pass through the main hall of the hospital which, most mornings, was athrong with outpatients; now the rows of hard chairs and benches were unoccupied, the cubicles for dressings had their curtains drawn back and waves of carbolic wash rose from the rubberised flooring and yellow painted walls. Off the Out-Patients' Hall was Casualty, and that was ablaze with light, as usual. Joanna put her head round the door and saw two figures on the examination couches being severely harangued by the night C.O.

'Fight,' explained the Casualty night nurse succinctly, as she saw the visitor. 'One has lost two of his top incisors, and he's only twenty-four. If I was his girlfriend I would break it off, so I would.'

'That's because you're obviously not in love, Nurse,' teased Jo, who was in love and was sure she would continue to love Nick even if he lost all his teeth *and* his hair. 'Tell Doctor Blake not to be too hard on them. I seem to remember that last New Year's Eve *he* had a little too much champagne and was offering to fight the R.M.O.' The nurse laughed and Joanna went on her way.

Here in the old building, the wards still looked cosy but the corridors were tiled and cold. There was a small area of heat round each old-fashioned radiator and then whole yards of chilliness. The Women's Medical Ward was a blaze of light and several altercations were going on when Joanna entered and said, 'Now, now! Ladies'—she looked round severely—

'what's all the noise at this time of night?'

There was a somewhat sullen silence for a few moments. Though it was only ten-fifteen it was a late hour in the hospital ritual. Patients were given their milk drinks at a quarter to nine when the night staff took over, their sedation, if they needed it, soon afterwards and by nine-thirty they were usually asleep. They had to be awakened at six in the morning to allow the night staff to wash them, make their beds and take pulse and temperature readings before the day staff took over at half past seven with the breakfast trolleys.

'Now, what's the matter with everybody?' Joanna demanded. 'Nurse——?'

'Well, Mrs Mayhew said she couldn't sleep, Doctor, and she had a tickling cough which awoke Mrs Denton and Miss Earl.'

'She never had a cough before,' said one woman sharply, 'and she wouldn't take anything for it. I said she put it on deliberately.'

'And while you were saying it you woke me up,' her neighbour complained. 'I've had a sleeping pill, too, so that's me done for the night. Sister won't let me have another.'

'I always seem to be in trouble,' moaned Mrs Mayhew self-pityingly. 'I tried not to cough, but I couldn't stop.'

'I'll see you get something for that,' Joanna said, and instructed the nurse to bring a medicine glass containing a well-known placebo, a coloured spicy water which gave the necessary comfort without drugging. 'Now I want to see all lights out and everybody settled before I go. I'll sit under the night-light for a while and you'll all know I'm there.'

Her presence seemed to soothe the women and Mrs Mayhew's tickle was suppressed in the warm glow of peppermint and cloves. By a quarter to eleven there was the sound of deep breathing and one or two snores.

'Better go and pinch those noses, Nurse,' advised

Joanna in a whisper, 'before it all starts again. Let me know if you want me.'

'Yes, Doctor Temple. Thank you for coming.'

She called in at Men's Medical, but all was well now.

'Mr Nutting walked in his sleep a little while ago, so we've put restrainers on him. If he tries to get out of bed again, he'll wake up.'

Joanna decided to join Bill Whitley for that promised cup of coffee, but as she neared Casualty, Nurse Dennison was waiting for her.

'Would you come and look at a patient, Doctor? Tell us if you think we ought to call the R.M.O. He was going out to dinner, you see, but we've got his number——'

Dick Blake indicated the woman on the examination couch in one of the cubicles.

'I don't like it,' he whispered, 'I think she's crook.' Dick was an Australian. 'Her husband's in the waiting-room and he says she has these attacks regularly. But she couldn't, not this bad, and survive.'

Joanna reached first for the woman's wrist and sought the pulse; it raced thinly, unevenly, the blood bumping over invisible stones on its way from the heart. She then smiled into the woman's half-closed eyes, which opened fully, looking frightened.

'Why—why doesn't it stop, Doctor? It's going on— so long. So—so long. . . .'

'Don't worry, Mrs—er——?'

'Cartwright,' Dick Blake supplied.

'—We'll have you settled down in no time. Don't talk.' She pulled down the lower eyelids and saw them flood a purply red, then she ran her fingers up the skin on the sides of the neck and found the underlying glands slightly swollen and rigid. She looked in the mouth and nodded to nurse to remove the upper denture. The remaining teeth were not very good and should be removed as soon as the woman was up to such activity; it should preferably be done in hospital under medical supervision. Lastly she pressed the fingernails to finish the first part of her examination and then took out her stethoscope. The beat of the heart was as confused as she had expected by all the physical signs of distress; the blood hissed noisily through the damaged valve like water struggling against a partly open lock gate; there was considerable fibrillation and a soft systolic murmur down left of the sternum. The lungs rang with the activity of quickly drawn, shallow breaths which seemed to create an agony peculiarly their own.

'I think a quarter of morphia would have a calming influence for a start, Doctor Blake,' Joanna decided, taking the stethoscope and putting it into her pocket. 'I'd just like to have a word with Mr Cartwright.'

The man in the waiting-room was obviously upset. 'Well, Doctor? How's my wife? She was so bad I asked them to stop the bus outside the hospital. She— she couldn't get her breath.'

'I understand she has attacks frequently, Mr Cartwright? That she knows she has a heart damaged by rheumatic fever?'

'Yes. She had to have her pregnancy terminated some years ago. We can't have kids. Sometimes she's really fine and then she'll tackle a little extra something and upset herself so that she has to go to bed for a day or so and rest.'

'What extra something has she tackled this evening?'

The man looked self-conscious and cast down his eyes.

'She was fine—real fine—has been for weeks now. We went to the pictures, as we usually do on a Friday night, if there's anything worth seeing. Alice enjoyed it, and we called in the Fleece for a glass of milk stout, which helps us to sleep. Then the last bus was just moving off. We—we—caught it with a bit of a struggle.'

'You mean Mrs Cartwright ran for a bus in her condition?'

'You forget, Doctor. You forget when they're all

18

right how—how easily they can get all wrong. I've kicked myself, sitting here. She'll be O.K., won't she?'

'I hope so. It's easier to trigger these attacks off than to stop them. However, thanks for being so frank. We'll have to keep Mrs Cartwright in for a day or two, you understand?'

'Oh? Is it that bad?'

'We don't want her to go into failure, do we? The damaged heart has been called upon to do more than it is able. Your wife knows exactly how far she can go with it, and I'm sure it doesn't allow her to run. She'll have to be quietened down under drugs and have complete rest. It's much better that she should stay. Now, who's her doctor?'

'MacFarlane, Abbey Road.'

'I know Doctor MacFarlane. We'll be in touch with him.'

She went back to the wife and found her in a state of daze, due to the morphia. The heart was still labouring, however, and the woman's face and neck were a uniform shade of mauve.

'I think we should call the R.M.O.,' Jo suggested. 'She'll need to be admitted. I'd better tell Nurse Andrew on my ward to have a bed ready. How about some aminophyllene now, Doctor Blake? Doctor Darrin will ask what we've done.'

The Resident Medical Officer, when he arrived on the scene, gave a third full examination and nipped the skin on ankles and feet as an extra. At a nod from Joanna, the C.O. informed his senior that the woman had been injected with both morphine and aminophyllene.

'Should do the trick,' approved the R.M.O. 'What else can be done to relieve the heart?'

Doctor Blake looked blank. He was only in his internship, but Joanna had an idea.

'We could do a venesection, sir. She doesn't appear to be anaemic, in fact the reverse.'

'Good! Bleed her, then. I'll tell Doctor Rivers. He's been dining locally. I have the number.'

Simon Rivers was the consultant physician to St Paul's. He had a smart London practice and also lectured the students. Joanna was Doctor Rivers' registrar and had always treated him with the respect one reserves for people whom one slightly mistrusts yet ambivalently admires. Doctor Rivers' cynical smile could put one right off one's stride and his humour often appeared unkind. He was possessed of a species of radar which could pick out human frailty a mile off; if his housemen were lacking in perfection he apprised them of the fact, usually in front of the whole ward, and his registrar could not afford to make a slip for she too was never allowed to get away with it.

Joanna felt she could enjoy helping Mrs Cartwright with the assistance of Doctor Blake now that the R.M.O. had approved her course of action.

'Need we bother Doctor Rivers, sir?'

'It's weekend, Doctor. He won't be in till Monday at ten. That's a long time. He would prefer to see this one now. But you get on with your blood-letting.'

This was not so easy as it sounded, for Mrs Cartwright had poor veins. As one collapsed after the other, Joanna said shortly, 'I hate taking blood from an artery. We'll have a last shot.'

The blood began to appear as she pressed the plunger into the radial vein and slowly crept up the phial.

'Take us an hour to get a pint this way,' Dick grumbled.

'Better slow and sure. You have another needle ready.'

Simon Rivers arrived while Dick was busy with a suspected ankle fracture; there were always customers in Casualty. Thinking it to be Dick behind her, however, Joanna said querulously, 'Well, you took long enough, I must say!'

'Twelve minutes exactly, after receiving the R.M.O.'s message, Doctor Temple. I can manage without your criticism, thank you.'

Joanna groaned inwardly. She was off on the wrong foot for a start. It was no use explaining to the consultant that she had thought he was someone else. He would probably flash that sardonic smile of his and say, '*Qui s'excuse, s'accuse*,' or something equally squashing. He took in the scene in the cubicle at a glance, lifted Mrs Cartwright's eyelid, which she closed protestingly, took her pulse and then complained, 'Aren't you making a terrible mess, Doctor Temple? There's an area of bruising as big as an apple.'

'I couldn't find another vein, sir.'

'Tut, tut! We'll find one somewhere if necessary, but stop that now, please.'

Joanna, battening down a wave of fury in her breast, began giving a resumé of the case as Simon Rivers used investigating fingers to do more or less what she had done originally.

'She's much more settled now, sir,' she said in conclusion.

'She's much quieter, you mean. I'm not getting a heartbeat and there's only a small pulse.'

Joanna's eyes were startled question-marks.

'Coramine, quickly! She's in failure.'

It was twelve minutes before the heart was beating laboriously once more and Mrs Cartwright was despatched to the ward to be watched all night. A nurse was asked to volunteer for special duty and Nurse Findlater arrived, rubbing the sleep out of her eyes and yawning lugubriously.

The medical team at last relaxed a little. For the first time Joanna noticed Simon Rivers was wearing a dinner jacket and looked most distinguished. He was the youngest consultant ever known at St Paul's, being about thirty-two years old and the son of a famous heart and lung man, now retired. The R.M.O. had pushed his grizzled hair up until it stuck out like a brush, but Simon Rivers had a thick dark thatch, well cut and brushed; his eyes, too, were dark. It was rumoured he had had a Spanish mother. There were many other rumours about him, though few were ever confirmed.

The fact that he was domiciled in London precluded the hospital from satisfying its voracioous appetite regarding him. It was said he was engaged, married, divorced; that he had been seen at a theatre with a redhead, brunette, blonde; that he was the only human being ever to get away with calling the P.N.O.—still referred to as Matron—an old cow, bag of wind, unscrupulous old witch. The rumours grew more colourful as they descended to the ranks of the junior probationers, who no doubt were prone to express their own sentiments when retailing what had supposedly been gleaned from the grapevine. The actual remark he made had been overheard by Bella, Matron's personal maid, as she removed the tea-tray after Matron had entertained him in her private rooms after a long clinic one afternoon. He had slapped his thigh and said, 'Dammit, you're psychic, Matron. They'd have ducked you in the old days for less than that.'

It was now a little after midnight and Joanna thought longingly about that cup of coffee she had been going to share with Bill Whitley. She wondered whether or not his tonsillectomies were playing up or if it was just the medical side having all the excitement. The three doctors were strolling down the main corridor of the old hospital, the consultant and the R.M.O. shoulder to shoulder, or rather head to shoulder, for Simon Rivers was well over six foot in height. Joanna brought up the rear, trying to catch what her seniors were saying in case she was meant to be following their conversation.

'So if you find me a bed I'll stay the night,' Doctor Rivers volunteered. 'My registrar is on call and you can then get some sleep, Darrin, as you no doubt well deserve. I know these rheumatic-fever hearts: they'll tick along like old clocks until they're overwound, then they cut right out in protest. Unfortunately, like old clocks, there are no suitable spare parts around.'

In a sort of dream Joanna had heard the ululating klaxon of the ambulance, and thought, 'Poor old Dick. There he goes again!' She passed Casualty, however, dutifully, with her own team, wondering when somebody was going to tell her to fall out and get some refreshment, but now Simon Rivers was speaking of a mutual acquaintance and urging the R.M.O., 'You must remember that paper he wrote on thyroidism? I must let you read it again.'

Running feet behind caused Joanna to turn round. Nurse Dennison, from Casualty, was looking white-faced and shocked.

'Oh, Doctor Temple, can you come, please?'

'Certainly.' She thought it must be her professional services which were once more required. 'Sir?' she deferred, awaiting permission.

'What is it, Nurse?' asked Simon Rivers.

'Car accident, sir. Nurse Frear has severe lacerations.'

'Yvonne!' Joanna almost shrieked, and flew in the direction of Casualty.

Simon Rivers inquired icily, 'Who is Nurse Frear? Why has my normally undemonstrative registrar dashed off in hysterics?'

The R.M.O. said apologetically, 'Nurse Frear is Doctor Temple's sister, sir.'

'Oh.' The cynicism was wiped from the handsome face immediately and a deep concern took its place. 'Then, as long as we are here, why don't we go along to Casualty and see what we can do? I'm sure my assistant shouldn't be allowed to deal with her own flesh and blood in her present shocked state.'

Joanna dashed into the cubicle where she could hear Yvonne blubbering like a child.

'Darling, darling!' she exclaimed, looking at the mess of blood which was her sister's face. 'What happened? Oh, my poor sweet!'

Dick Blake, busy with gauze pads and surgical spirit said, 'It's mostly superficial, Jo. It looks worse than it is so far. A few splinters, which will have to come out.'

'That's not so bad, then, Yvonne?' Joanna began to

23

sob in a kind of relief and nursed her sister's head tenderly, her own limbs feeling unaccountably like jelly. 'You know'—she said suddenly—'I do believe *I'm* going to faint. You shouldn't do things like this to me, sweetie.'

'You go and sit down, Jo,' advised Dick. 'I can manage here. Nurse had no right to frighten you like that. She's a tower of strength usually. I can't think what came over her.'

'Dennisons's one of my room-mates,' Yvonne tearfully explained. 'I *am* sorry, Jo, I really am sorry. You must believe that.'

'Oh, I do, darling. But there's nothing to be sorry for. You're going to be all right.'

She allowed herself to be gently pushed outside the cubicle and the R.M.O. took her place. Simon Rivers was holding out a glass of golden-coloured liquid.

'Here you are, Doctor. A pick-me-up. I hear your sister isn't too bad and the driver of the car got away with bruises.'

'Oh, yes,' Jo agreed, the brandy burning its way down her throat and arriving in a warm pool somewhere about her middle, sending out waves of comforting reassurances, 'the driver of the car. I really only had concern for my sister when I heard. Thank you, sir, I feel much better now.'

'Good! I think enough is going on here and I suggest you go and have some coffee. I will answer for Mrs Cartwright until you're feeling quite yourself again.'

If Joanna had not dropped her stethoscope and stopped to retrieve it she would not still have been in Casualty when a pair of curtains opposite were pulled aside and Nurse Dennison emerged, followed by a sheepish-looking young man with a black eye and a piece of sticking paster on his chin.

'I think you'll be all right, Mr Denham,' the nurse said with a smile. 'You're lucky to have got off so lightly.'

Nicholas Denham had sand-coloured eyes and red hair. He could not have passed for anyone else had he wanted to. He said lamely, 'Jo? Hello, Jo!'

She replied, 'Hello, Nick!' a frown between her eyes. Then she looked towards the cubicle where Yvonne was still having splinters of glass removed from her face, and back to her fiancé.

At first a block in her thought processes refused to connect the two, but she also failed to recognise in this man, hanging his head and avoiding her eyes, the lover with whom, in her thought-world earlier this evening, she had shared all the joy of planning her wedding.

For one thing there were too many people in Casualty, so she turned and walked out, presuming Nick would follow her. There was no echo to her footsteps in the corridor, however, and when she did turn round she saw him making off in the opposite direction. Her heart began to hurt a little, as though it was pumping molten lead and making a great to-do out of it.

She made for the junior common-room, where there would be solitude at this time of night, but she never actually arrived. Instead she began to remember things, bits of conversation, nothing much when separate but taking on a whole new meaning when they came together. Nick pushing her away from him, unfastening her fingers from his neck and groaning, 'Jo, we can't go on like this. I want to get married.' Yvonne asserting, 'There's just one snag. He's engaged to somebody else, sort of unofficially.' Herself saying, 'I can't help feeling sorry for the other girl, though. Still, you can't be one hundred per cent sure of any man until you're actually married to him,' and then Yvonne coming in again with, 'Being you, you'd disover some snag,' and then her tearful outburst of, 'I'm sorry, Jo: I really am sorry! You must believe that.' Nicholas's eyes escaping from her own were expressive enough without need for words.

'I've been a fool,' Joanna thought, not yet allowing the wave of desolation to break over her and carry her away. 'I've been thinking Nick was behaving oddly lately, because he couldn't bear to be with me and not be married to me. I was prepared to throw up my job to satisfy him and just be a wife. And all the time he was seeing Yvonne and not knowing how to tell me it was over between us. I was enough in love for both of us and I didn't notice, would never have believed, this thing was happening to me. He even lied about tonight. I could be given any old excuse. He wanted to go out and make love to my sister! They shouldn't be here now, getting patched up in Casualty. They should be dead!'

A great and intolerable anger flooded her brain momentarily; the passion that is hurt and wishes only to inflict hurt upon others. It passed as quickly as it had come, leaving her weak and drained and utterly miserable. It was she who should be dead, beyond all the feeling she knew must be in store for her. This grief that grew like a cancer, feeding itself with remembrance and anecdote, even with vain hopes that all might not be as it seemed, devouring the substance so that all that remained was the unhappy shadow of oneself, seeing the world through the distorted lens of a tear.

For the first time in her career Joanna ignored the warning long, long, short, short, short bleeps from the receiver in her pocket; she failed even to connect them with herself or to think of herself as anything other than an unidentifiable pain with the power of ambulation. Thus she unlocked the glass door at the end of the residents' corridor and passed out into the chill of the dew-wet October garden. The lawn-grass soaked her thin duty shoes, but she was beyond physical discomfort. She groped through the dark towards the wooden seat, in the shadow of trees, which overlooked the lily-pool. There were no lilies now, only a shimmer of silk-black water between the weeds. The bushes were ghostly with mist-blankets and leaves fell desultorily without the spur of a wind. All was damp, sad and autumnal; it was the fall, heralding the finish.

Joanna sat on a cushion of damp, decaying leaves, unaware of her chilled body, and waited for tears to fall. Instead her eyes stared, unseeing, into the dark of the now unknown future lying ahead of her. In that moment she would willingly have given fifty of her life's years away. Oh, to be old, with a life lived, questions answered, and no more need to be afraid of what tomorrow would bring!

CHAPTER TWO

SIMON RIVERS was growing somewhat irritable.

'Where can that young woman have got to?' he demanded of the R.M.O., who still hadn't got to his bed. They were washing their hands, having brought Mrs Cartwright out of heart failure for the second time in two hours.

'I don't know, sir,' Doctor Darrin said worriedly. 'It isn't like her not to answer a summons. She's not in the common-room and she isn't in her own quarters. I don't think she's the type to do anything stupid——'

'Such as?' Doctor Rivers inquired. 'Why do you say such a thing as that?'

'Because, sir'—Andrew Darrin looked most uncomfortable—'she's had a terrible shock. The accident, earlier——'

'But her sister isn't dead. She won't even be marked after a few months.'

'It's not her sister I'm bothered about, sir. It's what young Mr Denham's been up to which bothers me. Those two were together tonight, and I'm one of the few people who happen to know that Denham is supposed to be engaged to your registrar, and that he was also supposed to be doing something else this evening. Doctor Temple told me this morning that she wouldn't be renewing her contract next month, that she was expecting to marry Mr Denham, and though she wanted to carry on working, everything would really depend on him. She also, in conversation, told me that he was attending a lecture at the University this evening.'

'But he could have done,' Simon Rivers argued, 'and then merely given this girl a lift home from somewhere. It may be perfectly innocent.'

'I was helping clean Nurse Frear up, if you remember, sir, and was was somewhat hysterical. She kept hoping that Jo wouldn't hate her. "This seems like a judgment on me," she said, "for taking Nick off her. She'll think I knew all the time, but I didn't." I told her she'd better keep quiet about her private affairs and then she added, a little defiantly, "We're not ashamed of being in love, you know. It isn't like the other time when the man was married. Jo broke that up, so it's a kind of poetic justice that I should break up her affair."'

Simon Rivers looked at his watch and sighed. 'It's after one. I'm sorry for keeping you up, Darrin.'

'It isn't the first time, nor will it be the last, sir. Fortunately I can take cat-naps of five minutes' duration which always put me back on the ball.'

'Would you mind having one in Sister's office here, where Nurse can reach you, while I go and look for Doctor Temple? She can't have disappeared into thin air.'

Twenty minutes later, having discovered the garden door ajar, Simon Rivers ran his registrar to earth. Her white coat made a ghost of her in the surrounding gloom of the garden. When he announced himself softly, she didn't move, however, so he sat down beside her.

'I understand you may be feeling a little upset, Doctor Temple.'

'Upset?' She turned her head slightly. 'I suppose that means it's all over the hospital that my sweetheart prefers my sister's company? Upset is scarcely the word for the way I feel at this moment.'

'No, well, however bad you're feeling it isn't at all unique. The same thing has happened to me and thousands of others.'

'I already feel much better for knowing that,' she said hollowly.

'I'm not intending to make you feel better. My intention is to urge you to retrieve your dignity. You have work, which you have already neglected on this account. The R.M.O. at this moment is doing your watchman job on the Cartwright woman, having assisted me in bringing her out of failure once more. Life will go on for you, no matter how unpalatable that thought may be at the moment, but it may end for Mrs Cartwright tonight. Of course you're unhappy, and no one else can relieve you of that, but your affairs are not so public as you fear. The R.M.O. has kept your confidence until he was worried for your safety, and it's quite safe with me.'

'Thank you,' was torn from her. 'My sister said, however, that when she won her man she would flaunt him before the whole hospital. She'll proceed to do that once she's over the shock of the accident, if I know her. Her sorrow for me will be somewhat gleeful. You see, I was instrumental in bringing her first love affair to nothing.'

'I always flatter myself I'm a judge of character. I didn't choose you out of several applicants to be my registrar because of your pretty face or even prettier figure. I chose you because I felt you had the required mentality; that you wouldn't flap and that I could rely on you to hold the fort here. If you're the girl I think you are, you'll hold it for the rest of this night in spite of everything that's happened.'

She turned to regard him fully, a crooked smile playing about her lips.

'I'm meant to rise to that, I know, sir,' she told him. 'You're quite a psychologist. If you're interested, the part of your pep speech which stimulated me most was that bit about the pretty figure. Obviously my depressed ego lapped that up.'

'It may have been expedient to mention it at this moment, but I had noticed you were also possessed of physical assets. What warm-blooded male wouldn't?'

'Except the one I thought was mine,' she said bitterly. 'However, sir, you've made your point and I shall go back to work. I—I'm sorry I deserted my post. I shouldn't have allowed my private feelings to influence my behaviour.'

'Good girl!' As she stood up he ran his fingers over

her arms and shoulders and added, 'You're soaked and chilled. No doubt that brandy you had earlier will have helped, but I think you'd better come and have some scalding coffee. Come with me to the senior common-room. It will be deserted at this hour and at least we'll be in touch if needed.'

She had never been in the senior common-room before and its opulence struck her; the chairs were large and well cushioned and the carpet deep-piled, hushing the tread of well-shod feet. She knew now, as feeling returned how cold she was and huddled near one of the radiators, shivering miserably.

At the wall phone she heard the consultant say, 'Please tell the R.M.O. he can go to bed now, Nurse. My registrar and I are within call. Thank him for holding the fort and do let us know if Mrs Cartwright is in trouble.'

He had no sooner snapped the receiver back in its rest than a night orderly tapped on the door and entered the room carrying a tray on which was a large coffee-pot and a plate of sandwiches. Here, Joanna pondered, to keep her mind off other things, one simply raised a finger and things happened; over on the junior side one made one's own coffee in the adjoining kitchen and purchased snacks at the staff canteen. Well—her thoughts twisted back on her, despite her efforts—there was now nothing to distract her from working her own way up to the medical hierarchy; all she had to look forward to was work—years of it, right up to retirement. She might spot her first wrinkles here in this very room; it was even possible she could rise to be the first woman Resident Medical Officer of St Paul's.

The coffee was indeed scalding, and Simon Rivers stood over her while she drank three cups straight off. The furnace thus lit inside her sent out its radiant heat until even her toes warmed up a little; she had removed her shoes and sat with her feet towards the electric fire, which had been switched on and added its glowing beam to the comfort of the room.

After half an hour she began to feel self-conscious, however. This man must be tired—he was not expected to be officially on call as she was—and goodness knew what he had already done today—or yesterday, as it must now be. St Paul's was not the only pie in which he stirred his elegant finger.

'I'm all right now, sir,' she said stolidly, drawing her shoes on in readiness, 'or at least I won't do anything silly. I'll go along and take a look at Mrs Cartwright and then stay in the junior common-room, where I belong. It was very kind of you to—to take an interest and not be too severe with me.'

He noticed with a feeling of anger against Mr Nicholas Denham, gynaecological house-surgeon, that there were bruises beneath her eyes as though she had been physically beaten. He had noticed particularly when he had arrived on the scene this evening how her fine chestnut eyes had flashed in a kind of exasperation for words she had not dared to speak. He often amused himself by baiting her, enjoying this typical reaction of hers. Now there was only a dull ache about them, an acceptance that her world had been shattered.

With just the right amount of diffidence he said, 'I know you're off duty tomorrow, and you'll be tired. If you can't sleep it's understandable that in your own time you'll want to wallow a bit, but the next day you may want a helping hand out of it. If so, and you care to, come and have dinner with me at my place. I usually eat about eight. There'll be nobody else present and we can have a chat. There's no need to let me know. Just turn up if you feel like it.'

'Thank you, sir. Goodnight!'

He nodded in response as she left, holding the door open for her, then he went along to the R.M.O.'s private office where a narrow little bed had hastily been prepared for him. Although he was dog-tired he couldn't sleep for thinking how it had been with him, five years ago, when Katrína had said prettily and hurtfully, 'I can't marry you, Simon,' and gone out to what had been Tanganyika and married a forestry official within three months.

Though Joanna was relieved that on Saturday she was off duty, there was a snag in that she had no occupation to take her mind off her troubles. She tried to sleep during the morning, but it was no use; she bounded back from occasional drowsiness to full watchfulness in which she had to reassure herself that what had happened was really so. Nicholas didn't want her any more, he preferred Yvonne.

In the afternoon she went out for a walk; a strong wind was driving cold rain into lances of steel which really stung exposed flesh, and she pervertedly enjoyed the discomfort it brought to her cheeks, and the way it drove between her collar and the rain-hood she was wearing, making a cold trickle down her back. She had a cup of tea and a slice of toast in a deserted café, suddenly aware that it was the first food she had taken that day. It took courage to return to the hospital and face the sudden blankness of her future therein; she supposed she would now have to reverse her decision to leave when her short-term contract ended at the end of the month. She would have to tell the R.M.O. that as she wasn't getting married there was nothing to stop her considering further offers. . . .

As she entered by the door leading to the residents' wing a figure stepped out of the shadows.

'Jo, I've been waiting for you. You had me worried.' Nick's red hair was ruffled and his eyes looked pale. They always did when he was upset about anything. From a first wild hope that he had waylaid her to say that everything was all right and that he loved only her, Joanna accepted the truth that he wanted to explain and apologise. She was amazed that she could put on quite a bright smile for him; this did not reach her eyes, however.

'Worried about me, Nick?' she asked him. 'Did you imagine I would stick my head in a gas-oven?'

'No, no. Where can we talk, Jo? I can't have you thinking I'm a heel.'

'I haven't got that far yet,' she told him. 'So far I've been thinking about me, in all this. Foolish and egotistical of me, I admit.' She charged off down the corridor, her mac dripping, while he trailed behind, fussing with his hands and murmuring explanations.

'I didn't intend this to happen, Jo. I took Yvonne out once or twice when you were busy and she sort of grew on me. I never thought it would be the end of us, honestly. When I faced myself a day or two ago I knew my feelings had changed and I didn't know what to do about it. You don't know what I went through— how I suffered——'

'Nick!' Joanna spun round to face him, her eyes blazing. 'Don't ask me to be sorry for you in all this, please! You had a choice and you made it. I have none. Humiliation, unlimited, is my share of this horrid business. So it happens; someone told me it isn't at all unique; people fall in and out of love like dropping their handkerchiefs. Well, that be as it may. I think I still have shreds of my pride left and I don't want you taking even those away by yapping at my heels now you don't find me lovable any more. Go away and make Yvonne happy if it's in you to do so, and if we meet again please forget there was ever anything between us. There isn't even any engagement to break. We never did make it official, if you remember?'

She didn't remember much about that night, what she did or whether or not she slept. She was glad that she had to work on Sunday; the R.M.O. was off duty and she was senior over all the medical side with two housemen, male and female, under her. Mrs Cartwright was very much better and already wanting to go home.

'We'll keep you until the weekend,' Joanna told her. 'You're going to have to learn what you can and cannot do with that heart of yours. There's no reason why, within limits, you shouldn't lead a moderately normal life. But even I don't run for buses, and my heart is A.1.' Apart from being broken, she thought grimly.

She was actually sorry when she finished her day's

work at six o'clock. The evening yawned like a cavern ahead of her. Hospital supper, something cold with salad, did not tempt her appetite one bit. It wasn't as though the salad was really salad; it was usually just lettuce and tomato, and tomatoes were beginning to lose their flavour. Like my life, she again gloomily pondered.

It was then she remembered Simon Rivers' invitation and actually considered it seriously. At the time it was given she had only wanted to be left alone, but now she was finding her own company a little too much, her bed-sitter in the hospital cramped like a prison cell. He had said she might need a helping hand, and that was exactly what she did need. She was up to the knees in some slough of despond and no matter which way she turned, could see no way out of it by her own volition.

Even having had an invitation tossed her way almost apologetically gave a sense of purpose to her evening; there was a reason for taking a quick shower, dressing up in the mustard-yellow trouser suit she had only worn once before, with a blouse of chocolate-coloured terylene, the same shade as her eyes; brushing her hair until it shone and then deciding on a flattering pair of shoes.

When she was ready she felt confident enough to accept a lift with Steve Cherry, a junior house-surgeon, who was going past the station on his way to the cinema.

She had seen Doctor Rivers' address written down often enough, but had never been in the quiet mews, not far from Harley Street, previously. The bell shrieked through the tall, quiet house and light after light snapped on as someone descended to open the front door. It was the consultant himself, wearing a casual corduroy jacket, a pipe clenched between his strong, square teeth.

'Oh, Doctor Temple—every time I address you I think you should be an archbishop—how nice to see you! I'm so glad you came. This is where I live; where my father used to practice. Would you like to look around?'

She made polite noises of affirmation, feeling rather nervous now that she was actually here. She wondered if he had really been expecting her or was, in reality, secretly bored by the idea of entertaining one who could not claim to be scintillating company at the moment.

'This is my waiting-room,' he explained, 'and my receptionist inhabits this small cupboard—complete with coffee percolator, you notice? Half her time must be spent in making coffee for one or the other of us. This is my consulting-room, and over there my partner presides——'

Joanna, who had gained an impression of rich carpeting, gorgeous draperies and an expensive-looking décor, now said, to show interest, 'I didn't know you had a partner, sir.'

'Oh, yes. Clive Edgerley. He's a heart man. Very, very sound. I have my flat upstairs. Clive's married and lives near Richmond. You—er—understand there's no one else in the house? That we're—quite alone? My daily woman doesn't come in at weekends, you see.'

Joanna felt her cheeks burning.

'Oh, sir, I'm not sixteen. And it—it isn't that sort of a date, is it? You did tell me there'd be nobody else.'

'Right!' He led the way upstairs, waved her towards a utilitarian-looking spare bedroom and said, 'Leave your coat in there and powder your nose, then join me in the main room. I'll order dinner. By the time we've had an aperitif it'll be here.'

The living-room had 'bachelor' written all over it and yet it was very comfortable in a brown and bookish way. The easy chairs were dark, upholstered in leather with deep, soft cushions, gold-tasselled: the table, across one corner, was like a polished mirror and the dining chairs surrounding it had tall carved backs and cabriole legs ending in ball and claw feet. There were two pictures only on the walls, obviously valuable, with ornate frames; both were seascapes. The unoccupied walls were completely book-lined. A log

36

fire burned fragrantly in what appeared to Joanna to be an Adam fireplace. She said to her host, after looking round, 'It's a very nice room, sir.'

'I like it,' he smiled. 'It has to serve as dining-room also. I used to have two small rooms, both far too fussy, so I had a wall knocked down with this result. Do sit down. What would you like to drink?'

'Er—have you sherry?'

'Absolutely everything, but have a Martini to start with. This is very dry and will buck you up.'

She realised, with a sense of shock, that she had temporarily forgotten she needed to be 'bucked up'. Could this, then, be the outer edge of recovery?

After two Martinis she not only felt better but positively light-headed. She had only picked at hospital lunch, and alcohol on an empty stomach always had this effect on her. She was laughing rather hysterically at a medical joke she hadn't heard before when the bell once more shrilled through the house, making her stop short, still hearing her own laughter like an echo.

'That will be dinner,' he told her. 'I won't be a moment.'

He came back upstairs with a cloth-covered tray.

'There's a rather good little restaurant just around the corner. They very kindly send meals out to lonely bachelors like myself if required.' He put the tray on a nearby sideboard and examined the contents of the various dishes. 'Excellent! A little smoked salmon for a start, then rare steaks with asparagus tips and sprouts and sherry trifle to finish. Would you serve, Doctor Temple, while I pour the wine?'

Her lost appetite returned as she put the first forkful of smoked salmon into her mouth; the glass of Reisling was cold and clean and across its crystal lip she saw the Spanish-dark eyes of Simon Rivers regarding her encouragingly.

'Do you mind if I call you Joanna?' he inquired.

'Not at all, sir,' she said, thus keeping herself in her place. When one was a consultant one could afford to

37

toss Christian names around, but it did not work in reverse.

'Well, Joanna, I think we should talk about you and your affairs. How are things going?'

'A little better now, sir, thank you. I think I'm over the worst. Today I find myself hardening and becoming most unlovable; preparing for spinsterhood, I suppose. I can't find it in me to forgive either of them, especially Nick. Yvonne may not have known from whom she was stealing, though frankly I don't think the knowledge would really have deterred her, but he did know she was my sister. I feel horribly bitter about that.'

'Still, the whole business was a terrible mistake on your part. Denham wasn't for you in a thousand years. He's inadequate at his job, inept in his relationships and a total ditherer and shilly-shallyer. When you eventually fell out of love with him, as you would have done, it would have been the same old story, a brilliant career sacrificed to mediocrity. You're better to lose him this way, though you won't be prepared to believe that at the moment.'

Joanna, who had expected sympathy and perhaps advice, was decidedly shaken or she would never have made a retort, bordering on insolence, to a consultant physician in whose house she was a guest.

'Perhaps I should consult you, sir, next time—if ever—I receive an offer? You can then tell me if this one will further my career or that one maintain happy relationships. It doesn't seem to matter to you that I *was* in love with him, and that, made as we are, nothing else seems to be important.'

'It's very important if it works. There's no better conclusion than fine lovers marrying and carving a future together. But all lovers are not fine. More often than not there's one giver and one taker, and the taker always has the power to break the giver. It's an uneasy relationship at best, once the novelty has worn off the marriage. You're not going to sit there and tell me that all married people are automatically happy ever after?

38

So many folk still think that marriage is an open sesame to a place called Bliss. Utter rubbish! I now think a marriage carefully planned by intelligent people, who are physically compatible, has the best chance of assured success. Marriage is a serious business; it involves other people—children. Why go into it in a whirl of ridiculous emotion? Would you perform a serious operation in a state of emotion? Of course not. You'd be coolly clinical if you were wise, and know exactly what you were about.'

'You're a verbose advocate for platonic marriage, sir, but extremely shy of taking your own medicine. I observe that despite your intelligence and obvious physical assets, you are still a bachelor.'

He smiled his big, white-toothed smile, his eyes crinkling at the corners.

'Give me time, Joanna! I'm not exactly in my dotage. My theories have required thought and I have only recently drawn my conclusions. I fully intend to marry making an intelligent rather than an emotional choice. Also I must correct you. This marriage would not merely be platonic. My wife would bear me children, I sincerely hope.'

Looking down at her plate, Joanna said, 'That must be difficult to do without involving emotions.'

'Quite impossible,' he agreed, and she looked up again. 'Emotion comes into it, and affection, *after* the wedding, which I think is the best time for it. If affection and emotion were still absent after a reasonable time then one could intelligently discuss termination of the existing contract. It should not be difficult to annul an unconsummated marriage.'

'Well!' Joanna held out her glass for more of the Beaujolais they were now drinking. 'I can't believe you're serious, sir, I think these are shock tactics to bounce me out of my depression. No woman would consider such an offer. They prefer proposals to propositions and they like having their emotions involved. Have you someone in mind for this enterprise?'

'I had,' he smiled coolly. 'You. I've always liked the

look of you and thought, "Now there's a girl with whom I could live!" This was before the events of the past few days, of course. I wasn't aware that you were otherwise involved.'

Joanna had grown pale with a high spot of colour on each cheek. Now, in her confusion, she knocked over her wine-glass and the dark liquid lay in a pool on the polished table. She said, 'Quick, a cloth! I hope there's no permanent damage done?'

He mopped and said, 'I think not to the table. How about to you? Us? Do you now never want to see me again? I shall understand if you would prefer to leave my service.'

CHAPTER THREE

THEY sat either side of the fireplace; she was sipping a liqueur with her coffee, while he took brandy with his.

'No, I'm not at all annoyed,' she assured him. 'I still think you're trying to shock me out of the doldrums, but it's a most effective method. I suppose it's a psychological experiment on your part. One man tosses me over and it takes another to convince me I haven't got two heads or an unsightly wart on my nose. But such tactics could have repercussions you don't expect, sir. Supposing I evinced interest in this blueprint marriage idea? What then?'

'I should be delighted, Joanna, and proceed to get to know you much better.'

As he was still smiling she wondered if he was joking, but his dark eyes upon her own brought the colour once more flooding to her cheeks. She had a wayward, vagrant desire to feel his lips upon hers, wondering if they would expunge the memory of Nick's from her mind.

As though reading her thoughts he proceeded, 'Of course it's early days for you to regard anyone else in the light of a suitor. The one who is rejected in love is bound in thrall for a while, but there is eventual release, I can assure you. Though much store is put by love, it usually boils down to injured pride in the final analysis. Of course I wish to restore your pride, such was my intention, but I truly meant what I said about considering you as a partner in my own marital enterprise. I've always liked you, and your habit of flaring up or quietly smouldering when I become either pompous or dictatorial. I've even deliberately provoked you on occasions, though my pleasure may henceforth be lost in your ability to deny it to me in future. I've considered the approaching termination of your contract with some dismay, knowing that I will mind losing you for many reasons, yet I know I *am not* in love with you in the accepted sense. My attachment to you is on a mental plane, and the easiest thing in the world would be to make it physical. Not now. You're not ready. But nature abhors a vacuum in the human heart and I'm telling you sincerely you will rise again and feel the need for masculine attention. You will get it, too, being the girl you are. Young men are hunting for mates constantly. Of course you will be suspicious of their intentions from now on, doubt the durability of their declarations. One will surely say, "I love you," with desire as his goad, another may truly love while you remain lukewarm, history having made you wary of giving yourself. I don't think either of these would bring you happiness, though again I only theorise. While other young men may offer you their hearts, and all that this implies, I ask you rationally to share my life, assuring you that our relationship can only progress or be terminated by mutual agreement. I couldn't live if the woman who shared my name was either vexed or unhappy. My marriage would demand of me the degree of success I expect from my work. So there it is—I've laid the cards on the table for you to study.'

Joanna regarded her pink-lacquered nails with unnatural absorption.

'I don't expect an answer now,' he said softly. 'I won't even mention this conversation again. When you finish your contract you can either refer to it or simply move on elsewhere. The idea will either grow on you or not bear consideration. There are no hearts to be broken, so you can speak freely as and when you're ready to do so.'

'Very well, I'll let you know one way or the other,' she told him frankly, still thinking the idea too fantastic to bear serious consideration. 'You did mention the fact that my career would have been sacrificed had I married Nick, and you may well have been right, for he said one doctor in the family was enough. I would have fought him on this issue, of course, but the question arises how important would my career be to you?'

'Equally important with my own, and I could of course give you the benefit of my tutorship. However, you may be interested to hear I'm not happy in my present orbit. I took over where my father left off, but at rising thirty-three I think I've merely jumped into his shoes and I now feel an urge to live my own life and work where I would enjoy doing my job.'

Joanna said in genuine concern. 'Throw up your consultant's job and the medical school? What about this practice?'

'Edgerley is making a name for himself as famous as my father's. If I move out a young hopeful will be given a chance to specialise under him. I will simply draw my ten per cent and retain this flat. A *pied-à-terre* in London never comes amiss. As to St Paul's and the medical school, well, there are thousands of talented and overworked registrars just awaiting the opportunity of improving their lots. If you decide to stay on you may meet the lucky lad or lass who is appointed in my place.'

'I don't think I should care to see anyone in your place, sir.'

'Well, that's hopeful. At least I know you don't hate me.'

'What do you plan to do?'

'Work abroad for a few years, as I wanted to do when I qualified. I worked in a hospital for tropical diseases before I specialised under my father. I would like to put the knowledge I gleaned to some practical use while I'm still young enough to enjoy the sun and the scenery of the tropics.'

'And how would a proposed marriage affect these plans?'

He smiled broadly. 'Well now, if I married another doctor it would have to be a double-harness appointment, wouldn't it? How would you fancy working in— say—Tanzania?'

'I haven't thought about it. I suppose one would

43

miss all the chromium and tiles.'

'I think some bush hospitals are stinkers, quite literally, but they may have got around to chromium and
tiles in the cities. However, there would be plenty of
patients to make up for any lack.'

'Any special reason you mention Tanzania, sir?'

'Mm—yes. I have a friend out there, who sends me
long, descriptive letters. It attracts me because there is
not only the indigenous African but also the settled
Arab. Both have created their own cultures and ways
of life. There are also vast modern projects, Canadian-
aided and run. Tanzania is bounding ahead. I would
like to see it before it actually arrives. Anyhow, take
your time—think—and we'll meet again here, four
weeks from tonight, to say goodbye, or——'

Joanna suddenly jumped up.

'Gracious! That can't be half past eleven?'

'It is. Don't worry, I shall see you back.'

'No, sir, there's no need,' she said with a show of
independence. 'If you can get me to the Underground,
the last train for Branham leaves Baker Street at midnight. You have to work, too, tomorrow.'

Joanna never knew why it was that the minute her
head touched the pillow that night, she slept like a
baby. When Dora, the doctor's maid, aroused her at
seven with a cup of tea she sat up like one drugged and
had to remind herself of all that had happened during
the past few days. Her heart took the now-familiar dip
as she remembered Nick's defection, but it took her a
shorter time to snap out of it and instead she remembered last evening's incredible dinner-party and
Simon Rivers' fantastic proposal.

Fancy allowing one's head to have rein in planning
the most intimate human relationship of all! It didn't
bear thought, so why was she thinking about it? Still,
it did something for a woman to be told she was first
choice in anybody's marital speculations, or rather the
first for a long time, for the consultant admitted to a
broken romance in his own past which had been partly

responsible for his present unusual attitude. Then again, the idea of anyone throwing up an established medical career astounded her. It was such a struggle to make headway in the profession that those who had arrived were both envied and revered. Simon Rivers may have stepped straight into his father's practice, but his consultancy at St Paul's had been earned and deserved. Still, if it didn't succeed in bringing him happiness he had every right to seek fresh woods and pastures new. So, she grimaced, would she be compelled to very soon.

She was summoned to the Children's Ward in the middle of the morning to examine a child who had unaccountably turned blue. This seemed to indicate a heart malfunction, though this had not been reported when the little fellow had been admitted for a T. and A. operation two days previously. Doctor Rivers had not yet arrived for his Monday morning round; the R.M.O. had informed Joanna that he had been held up dealing with a coronary thrombosis while on his way to St Paul's.

Yvonne worked on the Children's Ward when she was fit, and the staff nurse looked rather oddly at Joanna as she asked to see her small patient. It seemed to her that it was a glance significant with knowledge, as though Yvonne's tongue had already been wagging.

Joanna examined the little boy and made arrangements for him to be X-rayed. She entered the details of her examinatioon on his treatment card and handed it to Staff Nurse Oliver, who then coughed and somewhat nervously observed, 'You haven't been in to see Nurse Frear, Doctor. She mentioned the fact to me.'

'Yes, well'—Joanna knew that she was expected to show some signs of resentment, heartbreak and loss, which would duly be circulated on the hospital grapevine, so she had to think fast—'I've been rather busy and I did know she wasn't seriously hurt, having been with her when she was admitted after the accident.' She thought a white lie would not come amiss in the circumstances. 'I was going to look in on her last evening, but I had a dinner date. It was after midnight before I got in. Anyway, Nurse, if you see my sister today tell her I'll be looking in when I can.'

She sailed away, thinking she had carried that off rather well. If Yvonne thought she had been knocked down she would learn that she was by no means out. The fact was that she was by no means out. Her step became jauntier. For someone who had been jilted on Friday she was picking up her feet remarkably well on Monday!

Simon Rivers was chatting in Sister's office on Men's Medical by the time she returned. The two housemen were lounging about in the corridor as were the occupational therapist and the physiotherapist on ward duty. All were ready for the main medical round of the week during which every patient was visited and those who were getting better advised about their discharge from hospital. Each Wednesday the Resident Medical Officer also held a round and Doctor Rivers came in on Thursday afternoons when he visited those patients only who were really ill. Thursday mornings he held a clinic. He would always come, if notified, to see an emergency case, as Mrs Cartwright's had been.

This morning Joanna looked at him and his job through eyes opened during that revealing conversation of the previous evening; it was a most exacting and demanding job; he couldn't have much time left for leisure after his hospital commitments and those of his practice, let alone his lectures, which obviously had to be prepared. He was a young man with a mature man's niche in the world of medicine. He had obviously concluded that, like Jack, he was in danger of becoming a dull boy unless he made a break for it and did some living on his own account.

Joanna's job, during rounds, was to be the consultant's right hand and lend him her ear at all times. Her hearing had to be acute to catch comments not intended for the patient. She had to be alert and anticipate. This morning, however, she kept remembering things which disconcerted her. The man who whispered something about Mr Jonas' blood-pressure had also, in a way, asked her to marry him. She was his number one choice, in other words. As she murmured, 'It was only sixty over forty last night, sir,' she pondered that being a first choice really implied that there were other women prepared to take on the job of being Mrs Simon Rivers.

She wondered about these. Of course he must know many women. He must be considered eminently eligible and quite a catch. His Spanish-dark looks were outstanding and yet he was inherently English in his speech and mannerisms.

A flash of his teeth came her way.

'Doctor Temple is day-dreaming! Come back, Doctor!' There was a laugh from the assembly. 'For the second time, what is the level of blood urea?'

She told him, hating herself for blushing. Could he have forgotten what she remembered so readily? Had he really been fooling?'

'It will take time yet,' Simon Rivers told the patient kindly. 'Don't worry. You're making progress and we'll do all we can.'

'Thank you, Doctor. Thank you. That lady doctor—the nurses—they're ruddy angels. God bless 'em!'

The party moved on to the next bed and gradually weaved through the acute chest troubles to the chronics over the way. Here were lifelong bronchitis with heart murmurs and wheezy chests, a couple of diabetics and three kidney disorders. Two younger men, recovering respectively from pneumonia and a systolic murmur, were sitting in chairs near the top of the ward. Both were given their discharges, which would take effect on Thursday morning.

The ritual was then observed in the women's ward, where Mrs Cartwright was told she might go home on Thursday if she would promise not to run for any more buses.

'At the moment you're ticking over like a young ath-

47

lete,' Simon Rivers smiled, 'but don't go behaving like one. Get her up tomorrow afternoon, Sister, and see how she feels.'

Again the same complaints only with individual symptoms; a woman with pneumonia who reacted adversely to that life-saver known as M. and B. She had been having a very bad time, but was improving slowly on streptomycin; the diabetic who couldn't resist gorging on the contents of pastrycooks' windows and had been brought to hospital in coma. She now opened vague eyes and observed, 'I been a bad girl again, ain't I, Doc? 'Arry says me an' my iced fancies, I'll kill myself one of these days!'

It was midday when the round was over and now Simon Rivers would visit his private patients in the hospital, together with his Registrar only. The two housemen hastened to carry out the consultant's wishes on the wards; a blood transfusion to be set up here, an injection given there.

'What's happening on p.p.s?' Simon asked as they crossed the garden, this being a short cut on fine days.

'Nothing much, sir. Lady Hadley complains of her diet constantly. Mr Weidler had a very fair night.'

'And what sort of a night did you have, Doctor?'

'Me? Oh, very good. Yes, I had a very good night, thank you.'

'I'm glad to hear it. Now let's put on our thinking caps and decide how we can disguise milk in yet another way which will please a greedy old woman who can't digest anything else.'

Joanna had confirmed her decision not to prolong her present contract as Medical Registrar. She had seen the position advertised in the *British Medical Journal* and thought it sounded so attractive that she was almost persuaded to re-apply. She heard it being discussed in the junior common-room.

'Alan Barker is applying, but the poor devil hasn't a

48

chance. The Board always prefer an outsider to one of their own housemen who has made good.'

'I was one of Paul's housemen and *I* got the job,' Joanna argued.

'Oh, yes, love, but look at you,' invited Steve Cherry.

'What's wrong with me?'

'What's right, you mean. You're a very pretty girl. That always counts with the old boys on the Appointments Board.'

'That's slander, and they all heard you.'

Steve thumbed his nose carelessly.

'Being a girl didn't make the job any easier. I'm fair wore out, as one of my ladies is fond of saying. Alan stands as much chance of the job as anyone else. Doctor Rivers isn't a bad boss and the R.M.O.'s a bit too easy-going for his own good.'

'I heard Rivers was leaving, too,' Steve announced. 'The grapevine has it that he's had a mild coronary and decided to quit.'

The grapevine always broadcast eighty per cent of fiction with twenty per cent of truth. If Simon Rivers had suffered a mild coronary thrombosis, then he had remained on his feet throughout; that bit about his leaving might well be truth, however, after what he had told Joanna.

'In fact,' Mr Cherry went on, his tongue in his cheek, 'I wouldn't be surprised if you and he hadn't a secret understanding, Jo. It's very funny you both cocking a snook at the same time, and all those opportunities you must have had for necking in his office!'

Joanna found herself laughing, though the colour flamed momentarily in her cheeks.

'Guides' honour!' she held up crosssed fingers. 'I've never necked in the office with Doctor Rivers.'

'I've seen Jo necking with somebody else,' volunteered Bill Whitley, the E.N.T. houseman. 'Of course I'm too much of a gentleman to——'

'Well, keep it up,' Jo said sharply, 'being a gentleman, I mean. I'm not necking with anybody at the moment, as you so crudely put it. How did we get on to the eternal subject? I never enter this room but what the conversation swivels around to sex?'

'Sex? Who's discussing sex?' asked a new voice as one of the glamour boys of St Paul's entered the room. He was Irish, black-haired and blue-eyed with a delightful brogue, and stood six foot two in his socks. 'Jo, Oi've been let down by a red-haired honey of a norse and Oi'm stuck with two tickets for *Sisterly Feelings,* Friday noight. Come with me?'

Joanna had always resisted making dates with Mick McDermot. He was unalloyed beefcake, an assertive masculine male who would expect his chosen companion to be a girl first and a doctor second. To go out with Mick was to ask to be kissed.

'O.K.,' Jo agreed, feeling an urge to be desired even if only during the time it took for Mick McDermot to drive one-handed back from London to the hospital. She was rather ashamed of this urge, and yet the woman in her was clamouring to rise, like a phoenix, from the ashes of a dead love. She had got over Nick, but this was the period of void when life appeared drab and as lifeless as a set leaf lying on a lawn.

Of course the date with Mick was a mistake, as she had secretly known it would be. He was all for going into clinches before they arrived at the theatre and she had visions of fighting him all the way back home to the hospital. The show, however, was very funny and relaxing. Each time there was a bit of love play on stage, Mick's arm crept round his companion, and squeezed tightly. Joanna began to feel as though she was doomed to be bruised all over. She grew rather tired of struggling for her freedom and was embarrassed and yet unsurprised when a well-bred voice from behind requested pointedly, 'Excuse me! I wonder if you would mind sitting apart? Otherwise you obstruct my view.'

Mick was all for becoming aggressive and turned round. He then said, 'Sorry, sor,' and his ears were very pink. Joanna had thought she recognised the voice and almost died with mortification to realise that Simon Rivers had been witness to all those squeezings and cuddlings. How could fate have been so unkind as to display her in a moment of weakness before such a Mentor?

She was very conscious of the consultant's presence after that; he seemed to be with a woman who kept addressing him as 'darling' and smoked Russian cigarettes.

The show was almost at an end and Joanna had nearly succeeded in forgetting that first embarrassing half hour when she was conscious of an usherette in the aisle whispering.

'Doctor Rivers?' the girl was asking. 'Would Doctor Rivers answer, please?'

'I'm Doctor Rivers,' Simon said clearly.

'Please could you come with me, sir? A gentleman has been taken ill——'

Joanna felt a tap on her shoulder.

'Would you like to come? You may be able to help——'

Mick muttered, as she stepped across him, 'Of all the spoilsports!'

An elderly gentleman had been helped into the manager's office and was lying slumped over a desk, breathing stentorously. He straightened as the two approached and made half an attempt to rise, murmuring with difficulty, 'A lady. 'Scuse me.'

'I'm a doctor,' Joanna assured him, and looked up at the consultant, who nodded at her. She loosened the man's high, waxed, old-fashioned collar and bow-tie and undid the top buttons of his shirt.

'Can't get me breath at all,' he wheezed.

'We'll have you flat on the floor, I think,' Simon decided, again nodding at his assistant, who took the man's feet, 'and meanwhile we'll give you a shot to relieve all that congestion.'

From his coat, which had been brought from the cloakroom, he took a phial and hypodermic syringe. He drew up a dose of atropine as Joanna observed, 'I see you're prepared for emergencies, sir.'

'Always,' he said blandly. 'I've only once seen a play through without having my services called upon. That's why I refuse to go and see that long-running Agatha Christie thing. I should hate not knowing who done it!'

As Simon's stethoscope crept over the old man's chest the manager tapped and entered his office.

'A message from Doctor McDermot, Doctor Rivers; he says he'll see Miss Carstairs home if you'll see to Doctor Temple.'

'A fair exchange,' Simon responded. 'Tell him, very well.' After a pause he glanced Joanna's way and asked, 'I hope that's all right with you?'

'Thank you, sir. I can find my own way home, though.'

'No doubt. Only this time I won't allow it. Well, Mr Wallace, I think you're feeling a little better now? Still, I'm going to send you to hospital for a spell until they clear up your chest for you. You shouldn't have been out in the night air with bronchitis and your heart protested. A week's rest will do wonders.'

'Came out with m'son an' daughter-in-law. Celebration. Seventy-seven today.'

'Congratulations! I'll just have a word with your son and his wife. Put their minds at ease.'

Phoning the ambulance, talking to relatives and waiting to see the old man safely on his way took another half hour and then Simon Rivers handed Joanna into the front passenger seat of his E-type Jaguar, which a commissionaire had brought to the front of the theatre.

'I told the hospital you were assisting me and would be late,' he announced, 'so how about a bit of supper?'

'Lovely!' she told him. 'I haven't eaten out since— since I had dinner with you, sir, at your house.'

'Ah, yes, that dinner at my house.' His voice was almost too casual. 'I think on Sunday next we're due to repeat it?'

'Er—yes. You did kindly invite me again.'

'Unless you'd rather do something else?'

'No. No, I'm not doing anything else.'

'Good! Then I'll expect you. Are apologies in order for my breaking you up this evening?'

'No, they certainly are not.'

'I thought Doctor McDermot was being a bit of a nuisance, which is why I spoke up as I did. Actually my view was not impeded at all.'

'I know Doctor McDermot's reputation. I shouldn't have accompanied him unless I was willing to play his kind of games.'

'Well, he's got a new partner now to play with.'

'I'm sorry. The young lady was with you.'

'I assure you she'll be much happier with that young man, and I'—there was a somewhat pregnant pause during which Joanna's heart beat rather painfully—'am much more content in your company. I'm tired and I find you restful.'

'I'm not sure I should take that as a compliment.'

'Believe me, it is, Joanna. Very few women have this quality, and I for one rate it highly.'

They didn't speak again until they were seated in a restaurant in Soho with gipsy music playing in the background.

'If I were a fairy, Joanna'—she laughed gaily at the very idea—'and could grant you three wishes, what would they be?'

'You mean if one takes things like good health for granted?'

'Exactly. Three wishes for things you haven't got already.'

'Well, the first would be a rather foolish wish. I've always wanted a gipsy fiddler to stand over me playing a tune of my choice. He'—she pointed at the musician—'made me think of that one. The second—to be honest, I would like a car of my own, and thirdly, I would wish for a son. When I'm thinking as a woman, as one invariably does at times, I picture myself introducing a great boy, bigger than I am, as my son, very proudly. Funnily enough I never see him as a baby.' Her laughter tinkled again and Simon filled up her wine-glass. Alcohol was loosening up her tongue and he enjoyed what he heard.

'Well, why don't we make number one come true right now? He made a signal and the head waiter came over, bowing to obsequious attention. Obviously Simon Rivers was well known here. Next minute the gipsy fiddler was smiling and inviting, 'What would Madame wish me to play?'

Joanna was so enchanted she could scarcely think.

'One of Brahms' Hungarian dances?' she suggested.

The music was liquid, soulful and then danced into an infectious gaiety which had Joanna almost dancing in her chair.

'Oh, sir!' she said when it was over. 'That was lovely. I hope you enjoyed it, too? Now you must make three wishes. It's only fair.'

'Right. A foolish one, a practical one and a hopeful one. I would like to have someone name a rose after me. How about "Simon's Beauty"? Secondly, I would like to answer the phone at five o'clock one morning and be told, "Sorry, wrong number." There's no delight like snuggling back to sleep again with an easy conscience. Lastly, I think I would like to kiss you goodnight, Joanna. You're looking very lovely.'

The colour flooding her face was now not altogether accountable to the wine. She avoided his eyes and he noted the long sweep of her lashes against the flush on her cheeks.

'We—we'll have to wait and see,' she said, with an attempt at lightness, though her voice wobbled nervously. 'I'm sure it must be very late,' she added guiltily.

'Actually it's very early. Half past one a.m. I think, for your sake, I must take you home now. I'm having an easy weekend, but only because you'll be working. I can't have my registrar falling asleep on her feet in the wards.'

As the car shot away through the now quiet streets

he remarked, 'I'm resigning from St Paul's.'

'Yes, I—I did hear.'

'I've also applied for a new job as Medical Officer on a hydro-electrical site in Tanzania. It seems made to measure for my requirements. Have you applied for anything else yet?'

'No. I thought I would take a holiday and spend all the money I've been saving towards my home had I married.'

'A jolly good idea. Er—if you *were* interested, the same company which may employ me also needs a woman doctor to take care of the women and children in the village.'

'Which village?'

'I don't know its name. This project employs a lot of casual native labour and their womenfolk come along with their cooking-pots and kids to be with the men. It's the old Africa existing alongside the new. I think women doctors are welcome in Tanzania because there's a strong Moslem influence and some women would rather die than be examined by a man. I can find out more about it if you're interested.'

'But I've had no experience in tropical medicine.'

'Well, instead of taking that holiday you would have to acquire some. I could arrange all that. The appointment doesn't take effect until the New Year.'

'Oh. You still think we should get married?'

'I told you I wouldn't raise that subject until you did. I would like to marry you—yes. I shall accept your answer to all these suggestions on Sunday evening, and if you reject them I promise there will be no ill-feeling on my part.'

'I shall think about it very seriously. One of the effects of my—disappointment has been to make me apathetic about most things. I really enjoyed this evening, however, and thank you, sir. I think I may be—waking up.'

'One does, Joanna. Take it from me, one does.'

The car stopped outside the hospital gates.

'I shall watch you until you're admitted,' he announced, looking very tall in the darkness. 'There's been a prowler annoying the nurses and I wouldn't want anybody annoying you.'

She felt a stirring of warmth for this man. Women loved having a protector. As nervously as a gazelle she reached to her tip-toes and pecked him on the cheek, and as she would have run off he brought her round sharply to face him.

'You remembered my wish, then, Joanna?'

'Yes, yes, I did.' Her voice wasn't her own and her heart must surely stop if it raced so hard.

'My wish was that *I* be allowed to kiss *you* goodnight. So——?'

She had thought to die, in this moment, of sheer embarrassment, but the muscular lips which found her own were gentle, investigating and questioning. As they brushed hers she felt the stirrings of interest deep within her and leaned a little against him. Next minute there was a brief exaltation and then a drawing apart. There was a deepening awareness of sights and sounds, the consciousness of something begun which, though inconclusive, had captured the interest.

'Goodnight then, Joanna.'

'Goodnight, Simon.'

She never knew that she had called him by his name quite naturally and that in so doing she had left him feeling happier than for years. When he thought of Katrina now she seemed very far away, like a figure in a distant dream, but Joanna, his registrar, was very much with him, and to kiss her had been sweet and exciting. How shy she was! He almost snorted as he thought how people went about falling in love. There was no need for all that. One just needed to apply oneself intelligently, as tonight had proved.

Each one of those December mornings, when Joanna woke up, she pinched herself to make sure she was not still dreaming. Her room was pleasanter than the one at St Paul's had been and looked out over well-tended acres. This was the Nestor Clinic for Tropical

Diseases in North Surrey, and she was attached to the medical director, as an unpaid houseman, for an intensive course in the subject he knew down to his fingertips. She found it all absorbingly interesting too, though the patients were a little too well-lined for her liking. In one room lay an Arab sheikh, an oil millionaire, suffering from the lifelong effects of bilharzia contracted as a child; there were several white refugees from the independent nationalism of Kenya, with virulent malaria and enlarged spleens; there was a Nigerian chieftain with amoebic dysentery and a typhoid suspect from India. Sir John also told her of the things she would meet with commonly which she would not find in his clinic; deficiency diseases arising from incomplete diets and trachoma, which, if not caught in time, rendered the sufferer totally blind. He drove her hard because there wasn't much time. On December the twenty-third his pupil was to marry the son of his old friend Jonathan Rivers, and the two were going off to work in Tanzania, which used to be Tanganyika in his day.

Simon, true to his word, had fixed up Joanna's pupilage under Sir John and had given her a platinum engagement ring with a beautiful diamond in a setting of smaller stones. Every facet flashed coloured fire so that there was lavender and pink and a cold blue all at one and the same time.

When she had accepted his proposals his reactions had been somewhat surprising. Instead of sweeping her into his arms and kissing her as she had anticipated, he had indicated that there was much to be done and settled down to discuss business. The London office which was dealing with applications for the staffing of the Tanzanian Hydro-Electrical scheme had been contacted and an interview arranged for Joanna. The job was hers within a week and then she was rushed off to the clinic on the same day she became engaged to Simon, which also took place without any undue ceremony.

'I think this will fit you,' Simon had said, 'and women expect such things. I hope you like it.'

She had said, 'It's gorgeous! I didn't really expect it, but thanks just the same.'

In rather the same way he talked about the wedding.

'I'm sorry it's such a rush, but I'll be relieved when it's all settled. Do you mind a special licence and a register office, or would you rather be married in church?'

'Oh, I think a register office. It's not as though——'

'No. Exactly. Very well.'

She wondered, rather unhappily, why their promising physical relationship had not received encouragment. In Simon's arms, with those urging lips upon her own, she could have imagined all sorts of reasons why they could be happy ever after in this unusual relationship, but all she was getting were the cold, hard facts of a working partnership. True, there was a lot of business to the deal which kisses could not accomplish. She had to have a passport in her new name; Simon saw to that. She had to tell her mother of her change of plans for her future and announce her engagement. Simon helped her with that and utterly won over Mrs Frear in the process. There had to be tropical attire purchased, both for working and for leisure, and Simon advised and criticised and approved until she was satisfactorily kitted out. Then she was taken to a rambling old house in Sussex and introduced to the retired Doctor Rivers as 'my future wife', a title which took Joanna by surprise and made the old man polish up his spectacles to see her properly.

'Well, my boy,' he finally twinkled, 'I wondered what madness had got into you, throwing the practice up, and so forth, but now I think I understand. She's charming. Charming!'

Now her wedding day was only two days distant and she felt naturally nervous. When she was actually Simon's wife would he still be cold, or would he then imagine he had earned the right to possess her without the preliminaries of normal courtship? They were to meet in town, at Simon's flat, the following evening, and discuss their final arrangements.

She looked forward to this, at the eleventh hour, with apprehension unworthy of any bride-to-be; even an unloved one, as she was.

CHAPTER FOUR

OVER the actual arrangements for the wedding, Joanna came upon strong opposition from her mother.

'A register office!' she snorted. 'I never thought when you got married it would be in one of those places; and without crowds of people, you say, which means that Simon's father and I are to be the only two others present! A real hole and corner affair this is, I must say. Not even your own sister is to be asked! Well . . .! You haven't got yourself into trouble with this man, have you, Jo?'

'Mother! Does everybody who gets married at the registrar's have to be pregnant? No, I am not in any trouble, only at times like these when I could scream. It's *my* wedding and I want it to be very quiet. When Yvonne gets married she will no doubt do so with all the trimmings you so obviously desire, but you must have already noticed that Yvonne and I are not much alike. Now, can I count on your coming or not? We need two witnesses——'

This conversation had taken place some time ago and now Joanna called at her mother's flat before going to Upper Hall Place and her dinner engagement with Simon. She was surprised to find Yvonne at home, her face still scarred but healing nicely.

'Well!' Yvonne sneered. 'The bride-to-be herself! Mum's at the shops, but she won't be long. If you want a cup of coffee you can make it yourself, can't you? I've just had my meal.'

'I don't want anything, thanks.' Joanna was surprised how coming face to face with her sister still made her recoil, as from a snake. This was probably a purely psychological reaction, for she now looked back on her affair with Nicholas with no real regret. 'Is it your day off?'

'No. I've been home all week. Apparently my Al Capone beauty has an adverse effect on the patients. I'm suspended until my scars die back. It may take another month at least. I don't really mind. Mum's a bore, but Nick still loves me, you'll be glad to know.'

'I'm delighted,' Joanna said drily.

'You don't sound it. Anyway, Nick thinks you might have told him you were two-timing him with Doctor Rivers. It might have saved a lot of trouble.'

'I was two-timing *him*?' Joanna inquired, a dangerous glint in her eyes.

'Well, we've concluded something must have been going on. You'd scarcely be marrying the man in such a rush, otherwise, and it's all over the hospital——'

'I'm not really interested in what's all over the hospital, Yvonne, if you don't mind, having worked there and seen how the grapevine flourishes for myself. I don't intend telling you any more than you know already about my affairs, and I think you of all people will understand my reticence.'

'You flatter yourself if you think I'm interested. I'm not asked to your wedding, so why should I bother? I did call on Doctor Rivers, though,' she added with a sly smile, 'and he was very nice.'

'You called on Simon?' Joanna's face was like a mask. 'Why? Do you want him, too?'

'No. He's not my type, thank you. I called with a wedding present, if you must know. He said he would put it in your room.'

'Well, thanks for the present.' Joanna relaxed just a little. 'I really didn't expect it of you, Yvonne.'

'You're living with him, then?'

'What are you implying, for heaven's sake?'

'Well, he said he would put the gift in *your room*. I thought it very fishy.'

'Not exactly one of the three wise monkeys, are you, Yvonne? I shouldn't really bother to explain, but as I've finished at the clinic, I'm spending the next two nights in Simon's house. He, however, will be at his club, which you can believe or not.'

'Well, if you won't tell people the facts they'll believe the fiction, you know. You came in at two o'clock one night, and Mick McDermot said you were with your precious Simon, though you'd started off with him. Whatever could be going on until two in the morning?'

'Some bacchanalian orgy, no doubt. Actually we were playing wishing games.'

'Well, Nick's glad he found out what you were really like. He said he couldn't have been more mistaken about anybody than he was in you. He said——'

'Hello, Mum!' Joanna greeted, as Mrs Frear arrived home. 'Is that a new hat?'

'Well, it *is* your wedding, Jo, even though it is only at Caxton Hall. I thought I wouldn't let you down.'

Mother and daughter kissed for the first time in many, many years, and there was even a tear on the older woman's cheek as they drew apart. 'Your father would have been proud—so proud. He was so like you—didn't care for a fuss either. We were married at the registrar's, too, because it was what he wanted. Be happy, Jo.'

'I'll try, Mum. I'll try.'

'If I could play "Hearts and Flowers",' Yvonne said unkindly, 'I would.'

Simon was always telling Jo to take taxis for convenience, but she had been used to tight purse-strings and it wasn't a long walk from Baker Street Station to Upper Hall Place, off Harley Street, so she almost invariably walked. On this evening, after that clash with her sister and the sentimental outburst from her mother, she felt restless and uncertain about the future. She had managed to raise a certain degree of enthusiasm for the venture at one time, but now her mind had been filled with new medical facts and terms during her crash course at the clinic, and she had forgotten how nice Simon could be when he was being nice, for he too had had a lot to do and arrange. It was as though she was setting out to meet a man who was more of a stranger to her than ever, and the idea of becoming his wife in thirty-six hours was utterly fantastic.

She wondered how many girls had baulked at this late hour and how they had found the courage to do so. It seemed that so many people were involved in a marriage that one couldn't just say, 'No, thanks,' without causing quite a stir. In her own case, quiet as things were to be, there would be Simon to be told, then the registrar, and her mother, who would inform Yvonne and various friends who knew what was afoot. How many people Simon had told, she didn't know, but as he was spending his last bachelor night with a bunch of fellow medicos, it was obvious that quite a few people knew about the marriage.

As she walked down Harley Street she asked herself if she was thinking of backing down. No—no, not really, she told herself firmly. It was just that leaping wildly into the unknown was alien to her nature which had guided her, so far, in a direct line towards her chosen goal, which was medicine. Even marrying Nicholas had been a deviation of which her inner self had not entirely approved, though her emotional involvement had shouted down all opposition. Now there was no emotional involvement, only Simon in the role of Pygmalion moulding a mate to his own design, assuring her that some magic spark would create the soul needed for the enterprise in time. Would it, though? And if not, what then would the future hold for her that she could bear to think about?

Simon's receptionist admitted her to the house. It was the first time they had met and Joanna thought her a very pretty girl. Why had Simon overlooked such a one and chosen her, Joanna, to share his life?

'I believe you know your way upstairs, Doctor Temple? We have a patient who has travelled from the north and may keep us half an hour or so. Time for a couple of drinks, eh?'

'Thank you,' smiled Joanna, and went up the richly carpeted stairs into the spare bedroom which had been prepared for her use. The suit in which she was getting married was still in its box on the bed. She un-packed it and held it against her for a moment. 'I take thee, Simon——'

She didn't know whether those words were used in the civil ceremony or not, and put the suit away rather impatiently in the wardrobe. It was simple, dignified, and would serve for other occasions, being a rich dark blue. Her hat was of yellow straw with a blue ribbon bow.

She riffled through her tropical kit with more enthu-siasm, envisaging warm moonlit nights and mosquito-netted verandas and native children being brought to her with umbilical hernias and clouded, sore, trach-oma-infected eyes. If it was just the work in a new country it would be wonderful, and she could have made arrangements for herself without having to get involved with Simon. It was Simon who was the trou-ble. At this moment she didn't want to marry Simon at all, and if he had had second thoughts she would rejoice and feel mightily relieved.

'Good evening, Joanna!' came from the open door-way.

She spun round guiltily, glancing once at his coun-tenance and finding it a closed book.

'Good evening, Simon.'

'We're alone in the house now, so can talk freely. Shall we go into the other room?'

'Yes, yes.' She felt unaccountably nervous as she walked along one pace behind him and started visibly as he stopped to allow her to enter the living-room ahead of him.

'I believe some brides and bridegrooms suffer an emotional crisis, due to over-excitement, in the days immediately before their nuptials. They become con-vinced they are not in love, have never been in love and will never be able to feel anything for the other party again. Fortunately for family life this usually passes with time and patience.'

Joanna sat in her usual chair near the fire and looked up at him.

64

'We needn't expect to suffer like that,' he said with a small smile as he poured drinks for them both, 'so supposing we speak of our own personal pre-marital maladies? I think it would be a fib to say we're going blithely ahead without a single backward glance or moment of doubt?'

'You too, Simon?' she asked softly.

'But of course. I have had my moments, but I have never taken a step like this before. I sometimes think I've gone raving mad, a conclusion shared by others, I may add! On the other hand, sanity looks pretty grim so near to being discarded. How about you?'

'I've had my time, today, to question my sanity. Also I've been well and truly rattled at home. According to Yvonne the hospital has me written off as a scarlet woman. Not only have I been carrying on secretly with you for ages but I'm now also living with you quite openly because my things happen to be here. Also I've worked hard this month against time, and I feel dull as ditchwater instead of as I imagined I should be feeling. Of course'—she forced a laugh—'I can only imagine what I *should* be feeling. I may be wrong. So—so there we are.' Her lower lip trembled fractionally.

'Joanna,' he said quietly, 'come here, dear.'

She looked surprised but never hesitated, going to him as he stood by the side-table where the various bottles were arrayed together with some very fine cut glass. She felt his hands strong on her shoulders drawing her to him, and trembled as she leaned on his chest. His lips were as she had remembered them, at first as though she was a new wine being tasted, then he apparently found this wine to his palate and drank deeply. She emerged breathless from that embrace to find herself clinging to his lapels as though for dear life. Her legs felt weak and incapable. She didn't resist as he swept her up and carried her to the large leather settee under the window. He ran a hand over the curve of her cheek, down her throat and over her shoulder to the excitement of her young breast pouting under the silk of the blouse she was wearing, then his lips found hers again and this time she stirred under him, her excitement and pleasure in the encounter matching his.

In her ear he whispered, 'Joanna, you don't hate me, do you?'

'No, Simon, I—I don't hate you.'

'I think it might be all right. Don't you?'

'We must make it all right.'

'This helps, doesn't it?'

'Yes. Help me some more.'

'You know,' he said at length, 'I think the sooner we are married the better. Your reputation could well be genuinely lost with more encouragement of that sort.'

At midnight she lay looking at the ceiling in the empty house, feeling wakeful but much happier. She thought about Simon and how he grew on one. This evening he had been so nice, so physically exciting and so entertaining in the nearby restaurant where they had gone for dinner.

She had asked him what was happening after the wedding and he had said, 'Wait and see. I may have appeared to be neglecting you these past weeks, but there's been a lot to see to. You'll understand how busy I've been in good time. By the way, I see no gipsy violinists in this place, so you'll just have to go unserenaded tonight.'

She laughed and flushed. 'I see you have a most retentive memory, Simon, and I must watch what I say in future. In any case that other occasion was unique and memorable. To repeat it would cheapen it. Good things should only happen once.'

'Like marriage?'

'Good marriage—yes.'

His hand had reached out. 'Let's make ours a good one, Joanna. A once-only . . .'

'I promise to do my best . . .'

Her last day as a single girl passed in performing the

hundred and one jobs a bride-to-be needs to do. She had her hair shampooed and arranged for a girl to come round to the flat next morning and dress it to look right under the yellow hat before she left for Caxton Hall; she went through her old handbag and transferred personal items to the shiny new blue bag she had bought; she stacked her supply of medical textbooks in Simon's vast library, remembering to add the titles to the typed list she found in a drawer; she packed her tropical clothes in a cabin trunk, carefully folded in tissue paper, and went through her writing-case, reading and discarding old letters and making sure her address-book was up to date. She didn't intend writing any of her friends about the wedding until all was safely over. Even now she still feared something could go wrong. She supposed that people who were in love to start with were much more confident at this stage.

She didn't see Simon all day, though she heard him down below once or twice. Today he had no consultations—that part of his career was over for the time being—but no doubt he had a hundred last-minute things to see to as well. She saw one of them from the window as she was eating a poached egg on toast for her lunch. A red Austin Mini drew up behind Simon's large car and out stepped the brunette who had been with him that evening at the theatre before they had changed partners. She was a tall, rangy, model-looking girl and wore an expensive suede suit in a mustard shade and boots to match. Her hair was shoulder-length and shone like black silk.

The visitor was apparently extremely welcome, for there was soon the sound of masculine laughter and the faint chink of glasses.

'A party?' Jo thought bleakly. 'Apparently I'm not invited.'

After a few more minutes she heard the girl outside again, but forbore to look.

'No, darling,' she heard her say, 'we'll take my Mini. It's so much easier to park. Fortunately I booked a table. You can drive if you like.'

Something inside Joanna, the existence of which she hadn't even dreamed, bit at her vitals with the sharpness of a serpent's tooth. Her reaction was to desire to hurl her lonely lunch-tray through the window, but she overcame this and swallowed slowly and painfully.

Could it be that she was jealous of her fiancé saying goodbye to his girl-friends? But what was to stop her phoning Nick or Mick McDermot and having lunch out herself? There was nothing, but she simply didn't wish to. From this she deduced that Simon did wish to and that she minded. It was ridiculous that she should be jealous of a man's activities whom she didn't even love.

That afternoon she spent at the hairdresser's so she didn't see the Mini return, and when she returned to the flat Simon's car had gone, as had Doctor Edgerley's Aston Martin. There was a light in the office where the practice's secretary was still working. She was a middle-aged woman with a nice little figure and bright ginger hair. She came out into the hall as she heard Joanna admit herself with the key Simon had given her.

'Oh, Miss Temple, the staff here have all joined in, and we want you to have this——' She handed over a dark box with loose wrappings. 'Do look, please, and see if you like it. It can be changed if you have any special colour-scheme in mind.'

Feeling a stirring of excitement, Joanna lifted the box lid, which was lined with white silk. Inside were six black coffee-cups lined with gold and six gold saucers.

'How absolutely lovely!' was torn from her.

The secretary looked pleased.

'Well, when I chose it I thought it was Doctor, somehow. We don't know very much about you, unfortunately.'

'I can assure you I like it very much, and will you please thank everyone concerned until I have time to write? I'll take it upstairs with me. I mustn't break it.'

'We—we're all glad Doctor's taking the plunge at last,' Mrs Holley said in conclusion. 'He's too nice to be wasted, and I'm sure you'll—er——'

'I'll try to make him happy,' Joanna said simply. 'Thanks again.'

She was preparing for bed at about half past eleven, feeling physically weary and yet so emotionally tense that she was convinced she wouldn't sleep, when the telephone at her bedside rang shrilly.

'Yes?' She didn't give the number in case it was a wrong number or a hoax.

'Joanna?'

Simon's voice. She felt warm within immediately and reassured before he spoke again. 'I'm at the Talk of the Town with a few other penguins. I wanted to call you, that's all.'

'I'm glad you did. I'm just ready for bed.'

'Hmmm! Don't misunderstand me when I say I wish I could join you. I'm really tired.'

'What's happening there? I can hear a sort of background subdued hubbub.'

'You're lucky. It's Bedlam in fact if I open the door. There, hear it? The first cabaret turn's just on, a sort of refined stripper. Instead of coming down to nature she's wearing a sort of skin of sequins.'

'Sounds interesting.'

'To a bunch of doctors? You must be joking. Edgerley's beefing because the ventriloquist who should have appeared is ill and this girl's come in his place. He says he's always loved talking dummies. The rest of my party are laying mild bets on the stripper's vital statistics. My own guess was forty, twenty-two and thirty-four.'

'Sounds a bit top-heavy.'

'Believe me, she looks it . . . By the way, what are yours, Joanna?'

'My what?'

'Vital statistics, you little tease.'

With a little bubble of laughter in her voice she said, 'I think you'd better wait and see. I shall pop a measuring-tape in with my hairbrush tomorrow.'

Very softly he said, 'You won't need it, Joanna. What do we want with measuring-tapes when I've got a perfectly adequate pair of arms?'

After that she climbed into bed and slept like a top the night long.

CHAPTER FIVE

IT was odd to think one was now a married woman.
Actually one felt no different physically, but mentally
the maturing process had been rapid. Joanna found
herself conversing much more easily with Doctor
Rivers senior now that she was Simon's wife. She felt
almost equal to anyone and wondered if it was true
that a man automatically either elevated his wife or
degraded her, depending upon his social position. She
felt herself to be upgraded somehow, and though she
wasn't a snob she liked the feeling and knew her
mother was swelling with satisfaction that this marriage was now an accomplished fact.

After the marriage ceremony they had gone to a
select little bar for drinks and snacks and then Simon
put his father into a taxi to take him back to the station
and the midday train to Sussex. Mrs Frear was dis-
patched a little later and then Simon regarded his wife
with a deep sigh of relief.

'Well, we made it!' he grinned. 'Now we can think
only of ourselves. Taxi!'

He still hadn't told her what was happening and she
felt little quivers of nervousness as he held tightly to
her hand in the taxi which he had directed back to
Upper Hall Street.

'I may say you're looking remarkably handsome,
Mrs Rivers,' he ventured in a Victorian husbandly
voice.

'Got to do credit to my husband,' she told him.

His dark eyes went almost dull as he regarded her,
but the kiss they promised didn't materialise.

'Home,' he announced later. 'How's that for size?'

She stood looking at a blue Sunbeam Rapier standing outside the door.

'Nice handy little car,' she agreed.

'Well'—he popped a bunch of keys into her hand—'it's yours. Try it.'

'Mine? This is my *car*? Oh, Simon!'

'Your wedding present, my dear. Wish number two, wasn't it?'

She emerged from the driver's seat of the new car covered in confusion.

'Simon, I haven't anything for you. I didn't think.'

'*You* have nothing for *me*?' He shook her gently. 'There's wish number three. Wish number three will also be mine.'

She remembered and panicked a little. She had wished for a son, and now Simon was her husband. 'So many things are happening, I can't take them all in. Please, Simon, help me!'

He was searching her countenance and now all her mental maturity had faded and she was a frightened child.

'Champagne on an empty stomach is bad for you,' he said in his normal tones. 'We're going to have lunch sent in and then we have to decide what's going on with us and what will follow after. You see, Joanna, we're sailing for Mombasa this evening on the *Chieftain*. I cancelled the plane tickets for next week and thought a leisurely cruise would do us both good. The people from the garage will see to the cars. They'll follow by cargo vessel. I hope you don't mind Christmas at sea?'

'Christmas?' she echoed. 'I'd forgotten about Christmas. My plans stopped at today.' She looked down. 'Oh, Simon, you've done all these things, made so many arrangements, and all I can do is fly into a panic. I'm sorry.'

'Don't ever run away from me, Joanna. I'm not an animal and will never hurt or trouble you, I hope; especially now that you're my wife.'

'I'm sorry, Simon. I do want to be a success.'

'It's a two-way thing. We'll make a success of it in time. These are early days and there's a lot to do. Now come and eat.'

After three days at sea Joanna felt almost calm again, fully rested and, it must be admitted, a little disappointed that she was still Simon's wife in name only. The fact that they occupied adjoining single cabins didn't help, but at the last moment these were all Simon had been able to get, and perhaps he had thought enforced propinquity might have proved embarrassing in those early days.

They had kept the secret that they were newlyweds most successfully; Joanna sometimes thought, rather grimly, that there was nothing to give them away, for Simon, though attentive, was never demonstrative in public and he was only in her cabin for minutes at a time, to have her approve the tying of his bow-tie or to ask if she was ready to go down to dinner; things like that.

Perhaps it was really her fault that there was not more between them. On their first evening at sea he had wanted to please her yet hesitated to intrude. It had been a busy, exciting day and they were still rather tense.

'I can't seem to wind myself down,' she had told him as they returned from dinner to her cabin, the baggage having now been distributed and needing unpacking.

'An early night is indicated,' he agreed, and looked round. 'Do you like your cabin?'

'Oh, yes. Thanks for the flowers, Simon. You're so very thoughtful.' He had turned to her half expectantly and she had raised her face to his. During that embrace, which was taking very good care of any remaining tensions, they sank to the bed, and then Simon had released her suddenly.

'Perhaps you'd like me to stay here with you?'

'Stay? Stay here?' Again that rising of panic in her bosom. She looked at her bed and realised that while there was plenty of room for one person, two would have to enfold very closely indeed. She said nothing and didn't look up at him.

'I suppose it would be rather cramped,' he said, and gave her a friendly little pat on the head. 'I'm going to unpack and turn in now. See you in the morning.'

She had a weep when he had gone. She felt such an inadequate fool. She was a grown woman, wasn't she? And he was a normal man with normal desires. She had married him knowing that she was expected to meet him halfway in making theirs a real union; he hadn't asked her to share his name that they might remain good friends only. He had told her, very frankly, that he was not interested in a platonic arrangement with the woman he chose to be his wife.

The next morning she vowed things would be different, but she was as mute as a dummy when Simon called in to say he was just going for a trip round the hospital with the ship's doctor. He didn't ask if she would like to go, and she felt rather miserable as she bathed and dressed and took a walk round the decks. The brave little ship was beginning to pitch a bit as she entered the notorious waters of Biscay and Joanna wondered if she might fall victim to seasickness. Her previous experience of ships was a channel ferry crossing to Calais on a blue, still August day with the sea like a mill-pond, so that wasn't really any test, and she had flown back from her brief holiday.

She soon discovered that there were other newly-weds on board, the Meakers, though these advertised the fact by doting upon each other every moment of the day and were never seen in the public rooms after dinner. Joanna heard about them from a garrulous female passenger who joined her on her walk round the deck.

'They're in the cabin next to me and some friends tease them dreadfully. They've had apple-pie beds, sewn-up nightclothes and the lot. The steward didn't get an answer this morning and four or five young men came and banged gongs outside their door. It's really quite hectic. Fortunately they take it all in good part. They're very much in love.'

Joanna felt as though she had swallowed something bitter and wondered fretfully where Simon had got to. She returned to her cabin, wind-blown, but he was not there, and when she shyly tapped on his door there was no answer. She threw herself on her bed, still thinking about the Meakers and envying them. Of course, theirs was a normal relationship; they had started by being in love and were behaving quite naturally. If she had married Nick she supposed the honeymoon period would have been quite ecstatic, too. But what about afterwards? Knowing what she now knew, that Nick was a shifter, the honeymoon would probably have been all that was good about the marriage, whereas Simon was a rock a woman could depend on. He was strong, thoughtful, patient and probably a little unhappy about her hesitancy in granting him the most primal of marital privileges and delights. Maybe he was thinking that she was holding back, being still full of doubts, to leave the door open for an annulment, but this was not so. She genuinely wanted to make him happy and wished he would assert his masculinity rather than pander to what could only be called maidenly reticence on her part.

When she heard his cabin door slam she was there in an instant and flung herself upon him in a kind of desperation.

'Joanna! Joanna!' he prised her free to regard her. 'What's all this, my dear?'

'I wondered where you'd got to. You've been away two hours.'

'I've been assisting at an operation. One of the crew developed an acute appendix in the night. I thought you'd have come along and asked for me. You knew where I was.'

'You might have been having a drink, or something, with the doctor, and I didn't want to intrude.' She made a genuine effort to get closer to him. 'How awful if I'm going to be a clinging sort of wife who can't bear to let you out of her sight for an instant!'

He kissed her lightly. 'I somehow think we needn't worry about that. You'd have to suffer metamorphosis, rather than marriage, to lose your innate independence.'

They were quite happy in their own way that day,

after Joanna realised she had to be intelligent rather than emotional in the post-wedding period, and get to know her husband better. They had long conversations about their respective childhoods and medical schools, sea air made them hungry for excellent food and they became friends with another couple and joined them for drinks in the bar.

'You haven't any children, Mrs Rivers?' asked Meg Rankin, with genuine interest.

'Not yet,' Simon said quickly, as Joanna turned away to cough in confusion. 'Too busy working, both of us. But we hope to have a couple, eventually.'

'I don't blame you waiting until you've finished your tour. This is our third tour and it's very difficult having young children in the tropics. Even if they don't get ill they become extremely spoilt. The house-boys unfortunately think a child can do no wrong and then the rascals imagine they can get away with any-thing all the time. I've been thoroughly ashamed of the way my two behaved when we were staying with my mother this leave. However, Billy will be nine next summer and then it will be worse sending him home to school.'

'I don't imagine we'll be doing more than one tour,' Joanna contributed, having regained her composure, 'so that question won't arise with us.'

Over the lip of her glass she suddenly met Simon's surprised, questioning glance and looked back again at Meg Rankin, who was speaking once more.

He had remembered her pronouncement, however, and mentioned it as they wended their way to see a film later that evening.

'Whatever put it into your head that we'll only be doing one tour overseas?' he asked her. 'We may like it and want to stay.'

'I suppose it was a hunch I had. Or maybe I really look on this venture as something you have to get out of your system, Simon; feeling that you really do belong to Harley Street with your talents.'

He regarded her silently for a few moments and

then squeezed her arm. 'Thanks for believing in me, Joanna. It's getting to be nice having you around.'

She thought determinedly, 'I won't drive him away tonight if he wants to stay!' and squeezed back to give him an indication of her feelings.

After the film show, however, she felt the old familiar nervousness his closeness roused in her, and when the Rankins suggested they break a bottle of champagne together, she almost leapt at the idea.

'I haven't had champagne since my wedding day!' she laughed, and looked up at Simon for approval of the joke.

After the first glass Joanna was thinking, 'This is all I need, a little dutch courage,' and she visibly relaxed as she sipped at her second.

After three glasses of champagne she felt wonderful and laughed merrily at every remark addressed to her.

'My wife is tight,' Simon said a little ruefully. 'I shall put her to bed forthwith.'

'Yes,' Joanna giggled, 'you'll jolly well have to put me to bed, too, because although I'm convinced I could fly, I'm blowed if I can walk.'

She tried standing up and lurched into Don Rankin, who said, 'Steady as she goes, old girl.'

'P-pardon me,' Joanna said happily, and then felt Simon holding her ramrod-straight and marching her off. She tittered a little helplessly as they reached her cabin and he searched in her evening bag for her key. 'I've never felt like this before,' she said, 'but it's wonderful. Why don't we have champagne every night?'

'Can you manage to get undressed, Joanna?'

'Get undressed?' she looked down at herself. 'Oh, lord, I jus' wanna lie down!'

She proceeded to do so, and he hauled her upright again.

'Joanna, you have to get out of your finery. Now, come on. I'll help you. There's your zip undone. Now, step out of your shoes and we'll hang the dress up.'

She giggled again as she obdiently stepped out of her shoes and lost three inches of height in doing so.

Standing in her petticoat she looked up at him. 'You're so big,' she murmured, 'and—and strong.'

'Everything off,' he urged, and she made a round 'O' with her lips and wagged her finger at him playfully. 'S'good thing we're married,' she smiled.

He patiently popped her nightdress over her head, picked her up like a baby and laid her between the sheets. She still kept her hands locked behind his neck and offered her lips for a kiss.

'Goodnight, Joanna.'

'Oh, no!' she protested. 'You're staying. I want you to stay. I'm your wife.'

'Yes, well,' he told her gently, 'you'll still be that tomorrow, won't you? I'll leave you to sleep it off.'

She sobered up quickly when he had gone. The champagne had made her gesture appear so easy, but he knew it was the drink speaking, and not her, and so he had rejected the offer.

Now they were standing off Gibraltar watching a tender take disembarking passengers ashore. They were also taking mail aboard and newspapers, the first for three days. All the men had disappeared behind the rustling pages of *The Times* and the *Telegraph*. The women had magazines and Joanna was writing a letter to her mother and finding it remarkably difficult. Already London seemed to be a city in another dimension that she had left years, rather than three days, ago. Today the sun was really warm and the air temperature was sixty-three degrees Fahrenheit, a lovely spring-like day for Boxing Day. Christmas had seemed unreal at sea, though the fare was traditional English and the entertainment festive. Today nobody was interested in food and Joanna had to confess that her only real interest was her husband. She now found she couldn't stop thinking about him, wondering what he was thinking and whether she had disappointed him in any way.

She found herself liking him more and more; she was proud of his looks and the way women's heads turned after him. He was so utterly courteous, too, at all times, and was the only man she had seen who hadn't deliberately avoided the ship's bore, who, despite an unfortunate impediment in his speech, insisted on discoursing at great length on any subject generally classified as dull or obsolete on which his own opinions were quoted as gospel.

The ship was preparing to get under way again and when Joanna saw Simon put his paper down she promptly discarded her letter-writing and hastened to put her hand on his arm.

'Walk, Simon?'

'If you like, Joanna.' He tugged her arm through his and they sauntered off. 'They've had a fall of snow back home.'

'Brr! I'm glad I'm here.'

'Honestly?'

'Yes. I look what my mother calls "peaked" in cold weather. Instead of coming in out of the snow all rosy and attractive I have a red nose and a blue face.'

'I don't believe you, but I meant are you really glad you're here apart from the deep and crisp and even in England?'

'Of course I'm glad. I like being with you, and I mean that.' She was looking down at her white sandals and he raised her chin up to regard her. Without saying a word he hugged her arm to his side, and a deep thrill of excitement ran through her being. She was nowadays so conscious of him that at times she felt incomplete in her own company.

She remembered apologising for drinking too much champagne on Christmas Eve, and he had said kindly, 'Well, at least you're cheerful under the influence. I've known some it takes the other way, who are positive wet blankets at a party. Of course I wouldn't advise too much repetition. You're inclined to love all the world while it lasts.'

'I—I wasn't so drunk as you may have thought, Simon,' she had told him frankly. 'I was tiddly, but I knew what I was saying. I asked you to stay because I wanted you to.'

'I'll remember you've just told me that, cold sober,' he had smiled.

'Do,' she assured him.

After proving herself as a sailor, for Biscay had been really rough on this routine trip for the ship, Joanna fell prey to a germ which was now affecting a percentage of the passengers and known as 'ship's tummy'. For a couple of days she lost all interest in living as her tortured stomach heaved like an animal within her, leaving her exhausted from its exertions. During this time Simon was a cool hand mopping her brow, a sympathetic presence content to sit without speaking while she dozed uneasily between attacks. Then gradually, with the tablets of Thalizole she had been taking dealing effectively with the germ, she began to lift her head again without the cabin spinning like a top about her and the first person she sought was her husband.

'Gosh, that was awful,' she sighed, 'but I'm feeling better now. Do you think I could have a little soup?'

'It's a good thing you decided on that voluntarily, my dear,' Simon smiled. 'I was trying to pluck up courage to force something down you. You were in danger of becoming dehydrated.'

'You need never worry, as a rule, about my inner man—or woman—Simon. I have a fabulous appetite and will no doubt become a very fat old lady in time.'

'Rubbish! You're a natural lightweight. Excellent glands,' he smiled. 'Well, I'll go and dig out the stewardess. She has quite a few like you under her care and will be glad to hear you're demanding nourishment.'

Joanna had missed going ashore at Valetta, in Malta, and the next port of call would be Port Said, with all the excitement ahead of a trip through the Suez Canal into the Red Sea and then down the coast of Africa proper. It was all so thrilling to anticipate, and yet she felt she was not enjoying to the full the pleasures of the present. It was not places which made one happy but people, and the person who loomed largest in her life at the moment was already on hand, serving her devotedly and leaving her when he thought she had had enough of his company.

A tenderness for Simon was stirring in Joanna's bosom, which she didn't quite recognise as the dawning of love. It was shy, for one thing, of making a claim on him which he might not yet be prepared to return. It seemed too pat to proclaim, 'Last week I married my husband and this week I find I'm in love with him!'

Her biggest regret was that he still seemed entirely self-sufficient. He couldn't have been more charming to her, but he was charming to all women; at times when she still saw in his eyes what he had only put into words that first night, he was not shattered by her lack of response. He literally smiled, shrugged and went away. Her illness had baulked yet again her determination to be a true wife to him and as she once more took nourishment and became herself again, she acknowledged a need to be rid of restraints which were rapidly assuming the proportions of shackles.

She decided to get up and go to dinner that evening. Simon was delighted.

'Are you sure you feel up to it?'

'I do. I hear there's dancing afterwards. Do you dance, Simon?'

'If one remembers it like bike-riding, then I do. And you, Joanna?'

'Yes. It seems funny that we don't know things like that about each other, doesn't it?'

'But nice, I think,' he smiled, and kissed her almost avuncularly.

'Not like that, Simon,' she protested. 'Properly, please.'

'Do you mean properly or improperly, madam?'

'I mean'—she reached up—'like this.' While she was doing the kissing he was obviously content to let her, but when she desisted he took over with a masculine concentration which left her breathless and a little dizzy. 'That's better,' she murmured, and wondered why he went off laughing, to change.

She discovered her husband was a very good dancer, that they matched up well in this regard. As the dance floor became somewhat crowded there was no excuse for taking up much room and so they danced cheek to cheek, and sometimes they were hardly even dancing at all but merely embracing to music. This idyll was brought to a sudden end by the arrival of the ship's nurse, a very pretty dark girl with rain-pool eyes. She excused herself as she tapped Simon on the shoulder and he pulled Joanna with him off the dance-floor to listen to Nurse Myers. He then turned to Joanna as the nurse went off about her business.

'Doctor Hennessy has got this bug you had. He's been staggering about all day, but now he's had to give in. The Captain has requested me to keep an eye on the hospital patients and be on hand for emergencies. I'd better go and let him know I'm agreeable.'

Joanna's first reaction was bitter disappointment that her lovely evening was ending prematurely and unsatisfactorily. She said, 'Oh, must you go?'

He asked softly, 'What do you think? Would you like to come, too?'

'No, I don't think I would, thank you,' she said shortly. 'I'll probably go to my cabin and play Patience, or something.'

He gave her a long, slow, assessing look and went off in the direction Nurse Myers had taken.

'It's not fair!' she almost wept. 'This damned ship doesn't employ my husband.'

She knew she was being unreasonable, that anywhere in the world people had the right to call on a doctor in emergency. She was a doctor too, and could halve the tasks requiring to be done by sharing them with him. A mulish determination to be aggrieved, however, made her desist as long as possible, and it was more than an hour later that she sought out the ship's hospital to offer her services.

Simon was in one of the small, dimly lit wards, and Nurse Myers was with him. She saw the girl's face upturned, laughing, and pretty as a picture. Supposing

Simon was human enough not to want assitance from his wife in these diverting circumstances!

When she turned away Joanna's heart was twisted with jealousy. She felt brittle and primeval and almost glad, as she was passing the ballroom, to have her way barred by a fair man with a sunburnt complexion who had become known as the ship's lady-killer.

'Dance or forfeit,' he murmured in her ear. 'This is gentlemen's request time and we poor bachelors at last come into our own.'

Joanna not only danced the request with Colin Aynesworth but every other dance too, apart from those they sat out together. He told her of his troubles, how he had hoped to be bringing a wife back with him, but in two and a half years his Linda had changed and said she'd be damned if she'd rot in any jungle. She said he had to give up his job in Kenya, buy a house in the London suburbs or it was all off.

'So off it damned well was, as far as I was concerned,' Colin said flatly. 'No woman should make a man dance to her piping. Does your old man come to heel when he's called?'

'I shouldn't think so. I haven't actually tried calling.'

'Then don't, my dear. It's fatal. Either he defies you or loses his self-esteem. Me in the London suburbs, indeed!'

Colin was drinking whiskies steadily while Joanna kept to tomato juice. She thought of her companion's warning and wondered if she could not learn something from it. Simon, she knew in her secret heart, would never be bent from doing something he knew to be his duty, no matter how unpopular he became by doing it, and it had been his will to agree when his assistance had been requested. She remembered that look he had given her, akin to the surprise with which a stranger regards an admired and pretty child throwing a disillusioning tantrum, and she knew she had been in the wrong to protest and that her protestations were futile in any case.

'It's after one o'clock!' she suddenly realised.

'Who cares?' Colin shrugged.

'I do. I'm going to my cabin. My husband's probably fast asleep by now.'

She had hoped, however. She would feel hurt if he hadn't missed her or tried to find her.

'I'll take you,' Colin offered.

'Oh, but there's no need. I do know the way.'

'Had the pleasure of your company,' the young man insisted, 'so must see you home, an' all that.'

In the fresh air of the promenade deck he rolled a little, however, and she had to put out a hand to steady him.

'Perhaps I should see *you* home, Colin?'

'My dear girl, I'm not a kid. I'm only happy at the moment. You should see me when I'm stewed.'

Somehow they arrived outside her cabin and she sought her key.

'Well, goodnight, Colin.'

'Goo'night, my dear, lovely lady. Goo'night.'

The fumes of whisky were overpowering and she almost fell through the door, as it opened, in sheer relief. The key had stuck a little, however, and as she retrieved it Colin stumbled past her into the cabin.

'Here, you can't stay, you know. It's very late and I want to go to bed.'

'Oh, dear! Lost me ruddy legs, temporar'ly,' he muttered, collapsing on the bed.

'Colin, please go. My husband——'

'Where's he? Where's his bed? Only a single cabin?' He looked round with interest. 'You don't sleep together?' he asked.

'Will you go?' she asked sharply. 'I'll have to ring for the night steward unless you do.'

'Oh, my dear Joanna, he'll conclude I was invited, won't he? We don't wanna sully your fair name. I'm a gennelman. Give me a hand up. Goo' girl!'

84

She gave him her hand and found herself unaccountably on the bed beside him, his alcoholic breath flooding over her as he sought her lips.

The next moment Colin jerked up and away as though he was a puppet on a string. He seemed to fly through the doorway and finished up in a heap on the floor of the corridor. Simon looked back at her as she smoothed her dishevelled hair and said in a voice which was at once a smouldering volcano and antarctic ice, 'Goodnight, Joanna. I think you'd better lock your door.'

She seemed to emerge from the horror of a bad dream into the nightmare of the reality, and far from locking her door, was through it as quickly as Colin who was now picking himself up, dusting himself down and looking as though an atom bomb had hit him. She tapped on the cabin door next to her own, seething peculiarly in her chest. There was no response, but inside the cabin a deep, masculine voice began to hum carelessly. Joanna tried the door and it opened. She put her back to it and her eyes were twin fires of pure indignation as she faced Simon in the act of removing his collar and tie. The weight in her chest was a physical thing and had to burst into words.

'Just who do you think you are?' she demanded fiercely. 'God? You came into my cabin, saw what you thought you saw, tried, condemned and hanged me without hearing one word on my behalf. Well, I've got quite a lot to say and I'm going to say it, unless you care to throw me out, too!'

He shrugged. 'At least you appear to be more articulate than your friend. Say on, if you wish. I, however, am disrobing and shall continue. I happen to want to get in my bed.'

'Oh,' she approached him, shuddering with anger, 'you're so smug, aren't you? You leave me to my own devices and automatically assume the worst. I happened to see you in the hospital with Nurse Myers, and I didn't think there was anything wrong in that.'

'I wasn't exactly in a huddle on the bed with her.'

'No, you weren't. And I was only in a huddle on the bed with Colin Aynesworth because he was bigger than I was and very drunk. You don't think I was there out of choice, do you? Well, do you?'

He turned to regard her, his eyes hot.

'I didn't know what to think. I wanted to kill him. I believe I was—was jealous. I'm not sure. I haven't felt like that before in my life.'

There was a long, pregnant silence and then eyes meeting and glancing off again as though not yet ready for impact. Her voice, when it came, was thin and high and the lump still in her chest was pressing on her heart and giving her palpitations.

'I—I minded Nurse Myers being with you. She's so pretty.'

Now there was the contact of eyes. They locked in a deep gaze of awareness.

'Perhaps our activities independent of one another are not so very important . . .' Simon hazarded.

Joanna leaned against him, hiding her face in the aftershave man-fragrance of his shoulder.

'I was wrong to resent your leaving me this evening, Simon, but I did, and there it is. I don't understand myself either, recently. I seem to have split my identity right down the middle. One half of me is doctor and the other your—your wife, and the wife was damned if she would let the doctor volunteer for duty, the way you did. I thought I was a very sensible person, but what I felt when I came in here was sheer nonsense.'

'It made sense to me. I was ripe for a quarrel. Sometimes a wife has to be a sparring-partner, too?'

'So that's why I wanted to hit you? But I only wanted to do that because I felt you should have known that drunken lout was forcing himself on me. I may have got myself a bad name back at St Paul's, Simon, but I don't play around with sacred things. Marriage to me is utterly sacred, and as long as I'm your wife you can trust me.'

86

He lifted up her chin and gazed down at her.

'The emotions don't think, Joanna. They only feel. Perhaps I'm aware of the first flaw in our arrangement and am peculiarly sensitive about certain things. I realise if you're not in love with me that it could happen at any time with someone else. Therefore it was a rival I observed with you and not a drunk. Do you understand?'

She leaned away from him knowing she had to find the right words now, or maybe it would be never.

'Simon,' she said with some difficulty, 'when I agreed to marry you it wasn't just because I'd been jilted and feared I might be left on the shelf. You'd told me you liked me and—well, that was a surprising compliment which did me no end of good. You were my boss; sometimes a bit of a bighead'—here he smiled ruefully—'and I hadn't thought of you as a member of my generation, quite frankly. When I began to I found that I liked you too, and I thought about you a lot. You grew on me very quickly because there's a great deal to you, and I haven't hated any part of it except that look and the voice which made me feel like a harlot a short while ago. For days, now, I've felt on the edge of falling in love with you, Simon. I don't know quite how to do it, but I'm not shopping around among the other passengers for what I know I can find right here.' Again she blundered against him, her cheeks scarlet. 'Oh, Simon, don't you know what I'm trying to say? I'm your wife! I'm your wife!'

She felt his body trembling against hers.

'I—I don't want to do anything we may regret, Joanna. You—you didn't want me that first night, remember?'

'Simon, my dear, I was nervous. I'm still nervous, but if we never get to know one another better we'll be frustrated and unhappy, which is worse.'

'Oh, Joanna!' They sank to the bed, shaking and laughing with emotion. 'I'm sure there's really nothing to be nervous about. Let's start with what we know.'

As soon as their lips met in the intensity of their desire one to give joy to the other, there was no need for instruction. Nature led them down the primrose paths of promised delight until Joanna, who had enjoyed her awakening sensuality passively at first, stirred into a sudden fever of desire which ignited her partner into a conflagration which burned briefly and satisfactorily and left them both spent and utterly content.

Sleep was the natural consequence of events, but Joanna couldn't forget the wonder of what had been and preferred to lie awake, knowing she had been transformed into a real woman by this man who still lay entwined in her arms, slumbering deeply. Passion slept too, but truth was always wakeful. Now she knew she loved Simon Rivers as she had never loved Nicholas Denham. Here was the substance where there had been only the shadow; here was the reality where there had only been the promise, and a broken promise at that. When Simon stirred she was waiting expectantly, and when he loved her again she felt her cup of joy run over.

When she met the Meakers on deck next day, while Simon was doing his hospital rounds, she smiled on another happy bride with a warmth of fellow-feeling which is said to make us wondrous kind one to another.

CHAPTER SIX

JOANNA hadn't believed such happiness possible as she experienced during the remainder of that enchanted voyage. It was not that the secrets of Eve became the be-all and end-all of her existence with Simon, but they certainly did help. They called passion as the handmaiden to serve the cause of their marriage and not as a master to hold them in thrall. They considered themselves very wise and most unusual, as do most lovers. Surely no others felt quite like they did? Such a treasure of delight could not be commonplace?

Once only, Simon spoke of a possible consequence of their mutual pleasure in each other, and once only.

'Joanna, you know the ropes. There isn't a doctor who doesn't. I'll leave it to you to decide when you want to be a mama, and in the meanwhile do whatever's necessary outside of keeping me away from you, which would be impossible.'

They were both blushing, but shyly rather than in embarrassment.

'I suppose I should have been very professional,' she admitted, 'but I haven't given such things a thought. It was you who said emotion didn't think, I believe?'

He rubbed her nose with his own, a gesture of pure affection. 'You don't think you could be—already?'

'No.' Was he just a little disappointed? 'I hardly think I would be received with open arms at our destination if I'm already pregnant, do you? Maybe after a year I'll consider I've earned the right to follow my inclinations at this moment.' She pushed him away, laughing breathlessly, as his inclinations were so obviously in sympathy with her own. 'Do you want children, Simon?'

'More than anything. I always have. I must get that from my mama, who as you know was Spanish and a great believer in families.'

A strange little pain gripped Joanna's heart temporarily as she pondered that his children had always been real to Simon. She, who would be their mother, God willing, was merely incidental in his plans.

She shook off this alien thought with the observation, 'If your mother wanted a family why did she have only one child?'

'That was a great disappointment to her. She tried, poor soul, and died after a third miscarriage. I hope you're sound and healthy, Joanna? I don't think I could go through what my father endured.'

'It could have been the Rhesus factor with your parents. How do we know that we——'

'We're both group "O", Rhesus positive. Nothing to worry about.'

'You mean you checked up on me?'

'When I was planning to ask you to be my wife I wanted to make a success of the venture, naturally. I made as sure as possible that we wouldn't fail one another. Do you mind, Joanna? Oh, my dear, don't be upset about it. I wasn't as sure of myself in those days and I didn't fancy you blaming me if you wanted children and there was anything to prevent us having them. It was better to be sure. Don't you agree?'

'I feel like part of a blueprint.'

'You're being silly. The blueprint went out of the porthole that night we had our row. Since then I haven't been steering at all and I've managed to be very, very happy. Don't spoil it, Joanna.'

'Oh, Simon, I'm sorry. I think when something's too perfect we deliberately introduce imperfection. I'm happy, too, and I can't always believe it's true. Being silly is my way of pinching myself.'

The ship cruised through the Suez Canal with the timeless Sinai desert on either side; roped camels stepped haughtily alongside military convoys and fast, dust-raising cars on the roads running parallel. The canal was much narrower than Joanna had imagined, and often a ship had to heave-to while another eased past. Passengers were inclined to segregate themselves to their own ships and scarcely a word was exchanged by people on the promenade deck of one vessel as they passed within four feet of those on another.

The *Chieftain* passed out of the canal into the waters of the Red Sea, and whereas temperatures to date had been tolerable, akin to European summer standards, it was now hot and very humid with a breeze blowing straight from Arabia, without any refreshment in it. Now everyone wore the minimum of clothing and there was talk of 'Getting back to work', or just 'Starting work', if the conversationalists were newcomers to East Africa.

Even Simon and Joanna began to read the literature of their joint appointments with greater interest. 'I wonder what our bungalow will be like?' Joanna wanted to know. 'I see we are allowed three servants, but I do hope I'll be able to cook for you sometimes.'

'As mistress of the house you'll do exactly as you like, my dear. But don't forget you'll be doing a job of work and may find you get tired easily until you're acclimatised. We'll see a bit of Kenya before arriving at Katsungi, which is only a hundred miles over the Tanzanian border. Beginning to feel excited?'

'Very. Though this voyage has been wonderful I'm wanting to get to work. Are you?'

'Yes. One can only enjoy so much leisure. I've no doubt after six months we'll be singing a very different tune, however.'

They both laughed.

'Simon . . .'

'Yes, Joanna?'

'You once told me your decision to come out to Tanzania was encouraged by a friend of yours already in the country, who wrote you long, descriptive letters. Will we be seeing him when we arrive?'

'Actually, it's "her", and I shouldn't think so. She's in the south, not far from Dar-es-Salaam.'

'Oh.' She minded knowing this friend of Simon's was a woman. 'Is she a friend of the family or something?'

'No.' He wondered if she was ready for the telling. 'She was the one who—who didn't want to marry me. I told you.'

'You mean the one you were in love with?'

'That's right. A long time ago.'

She gave a funny little laugh without mirth in it.

'How is it you're going out to be near her again?'

'I've told you we won't be near her. Tanzania's a big country.'

'But it seems funny you picked this job in the same country your—er—friend came to. You could have gone to the Congo or—or Kenya or Zambia.'

'Very true. I happened to like the sound of this job. Am I to be cross-examined on this account?'

She was stung, once more unsure of herself and him.

'I only think it's all very odd. I left my ex-boyfriend behind and I certainly didn't know we were coming out to be with your old lady-friend.' He sighed harshly and she knew this was the beginning of nagging in her. 'I don't care how big the country is. One has only to get on an aeroplane or a train and bingo!'

'Aren't you forgetting the fact that I've married you? I would scarcely have done that if my intention had been to carry on an intrigue with Katrina, who, I may add, has now been married for six years.'

'I'm being silly again, aren't I?'

'Of course you are. We belong to each other now. There's no room for third parties in our lives.'

There were now two little parachute seeds flying round in the ether, however, ready to sow themselves in Joanna's mind if she allowed them to take root. One was the fact that Simon had checked up on her physical ability to be his mate and the other was the knowledge that he had once loved and lost and the object of this initial devotion would soon be closer to him than she had been for years.

If only she could be convinced that all she had been to Simon had made him love her, no cloud would have dimmed the sky of her happiness, but even in their most intimate encounters he had never breathed those precious three words or called her 'darling!' It was as though he was always in control, even at times when she was not. She made him happy, but he was never a little crazy, as she was at times; he indulged her and enjoyed her, but she was sure that she was the one who was in love and that it hadn't yet happened to him—quite.

She was entirely mistaken, of course. Simon Rivers had known he was in love with his wife when he had seen that blond fellow assaulting her. There had been murder in his heart and a terrible fear that he had failed her, thus making her look elsewhere. Her declarations to the contrary had made him happier than he had expected to be again in his life; he had been full of theories as to how an ideal mating could become a love affair, but they had only been theories and needed to be proved. When Joanna had told him she was on the edge of falling in love with him he had felt like any young man driving a fast car for the first time; if he pressed too hard on the accelerator there could be a disaster; if he dallied he could appear a dull fellow. When, so easily, they seemed to be attuned, to really belong, he wanted to cry out his praises of his beloved, pour out his heart's worship, but he could not put what he felt into words. He had poured many words out to Katrina, who took them all as her due, and nowadays he could only vaguely remember her beautiful, madonna-like face, as though it was a mask she wore.

He couldn't remember why he had thought he loved her. He wanted to convey an impression of permanence to Joanna, not merely to pour banal phrases into the cornucopia of their loving when they were emotional together. 'Darling' was a word he tried to avoid, deciding it was tossed around too lightly among his contemporaries to retain much sentimental meaning.

Because he loved he was easily hurt on occasions when he fancied Joanna was lacking in trust. He could be in the same room with Katrina nowadays, and never take his eyes off his wife. Didn't she know that he had been surrounded by attractive women for years and yet known the brown-eyed girl with the blonde hair who became his registrar had more appeal for him in one defiant glare than they had with all their honeyed compliments and kittenish cavortings?

'If only' could well have finished the story of Simon and Joanna within a paragraph. If only Simon had realised that any woman needs to be told that she is beloved, in words, no matter how repetitive, or insincere the person who speaks them. 'I love you' does more for a woman than a whole day spent in a beauty parlour. If only Joanna had appreciated the compliment of a man like Simon offering her his life, rather than his love, initially, then all would have been well.

Like the woman who wished for a chimney, however, before she even had a house, she was inclined to forget that she possessed the substance while secretly fretting for the frills. Their love was too new and self-conscious, too diligent of letting others see. They had all they needed for perfect happiness, yet the same ingredients, wrongly mixed, could bring about a very different conclusion, and this was the threat hanging over the Rivers as they watched Mombasa rear out of the heat-haze, dusty and a little squalid and very, very hot.

'We're here,' Simon announced, regarding his wife in his usual wonder, dressed for going ashore in a cream-silk suit and large straw hat. 'Katsungi, here we come!'

'Here we come!' Joanna echoed, and found her hand reaching out for some kind of reassurance. Simon, who was saying goodbye to the Rankins, who were going on to Beira, didn't notice the gesture, however, and she promptly misunderstood by deciding he didn't like to be seen holding hands in public. Her first steps on African soil, therefore, were hesitant and dubious as she wondered at the ease with which she could now be hurt, and how there was nothing she seemed able to do about it.

The Canuck Club in Dar-es-Salaam was not simply another pre-cast concrete cube with windows. As it had been designed by a Canadian architect for the use of Canadian engineers and scientists, their wives and children, it was a wonderful building indeed, always cool to the point of chilliness after the heat of the Hades out of doors, though one quickly became accustomed to this and grateful for it. It was built round a swimming-pool, and there was a poolside bar and another up near the games-room, where one could play billiards or darts or table-tennis. It had its own landing for small yachts and speedboats; it loaned out skin-diving equipment for those who preferred to adventure in the waters of the Indian Ocean; it provided a nursery for the visiting under-fives and a full-time R.N. in charge of it. Membership was expensive, of course, but Canadians were used to good living, and where they served abroad, in their various capacities, and found things not quite to their liking, they were quick to provide their own facilities for both pleasure and leisure.

Katrina MacDonald, who had married a Canadian forestry official, and therefore was a legitimate member of the club, sat in a lounging-chair on an enclosed, air-conditioned veranda and gazed out at the yachts skimming like swans over the green silk of the sea. She didn't actually see them, for her thoughts were turned inward. Yesterday's row with Howard had been bitter and acrimonious. She had felt she hated him, and how she had learned to hate this damned country with its smells and flies, its climate which turned one's skin into leather unless one was shrouded from the sun at all times, and its sheer inefficiency. Howard would say they were learning, that it was a case of slowly, slowly catchee monkey, but it was too slow for Katrina, who ached for big city life

95

after six years and hadn't been able to bear it when Howard said he had signed on for yet another tour of duty.

'We'll go home for leave, honey,' he had told her—'home' was a suburb of Toronto—'then we'll come back for just one more spell.'

Katrina had already been 'home' to Toronto and met Howard's family, his parents and sisters who were open and friendly and didn't quite understand their sister-in-law from London, England.

Katrina felt she must go mad unless she could get away from Howard and the glaring mistake their marriage had been. She had left him a note back at the bungalow telling him she was rather fed-up and was having a couple of days at the club. He would know this was her way of rebelling at the prospect of another tour. She had occasionally thought of starting an affair with some unattached, husky male with a view to forcing Howard to consider divorcing her. The only thing that stayed her was that Howard was given to violence. If she had such an affair, and it came to his ears, he would deal out his own primal vengeance before turning to the courts, and Katrina was a physical coward, which was why she had always refused to have any children.

She began to think back to the days when she had been a nurse at a select London clinic, and had met Simon Rivers, who had fallen head over heels in love with her. Who could have known that Simon would do so well so early in his life? She had rejected him because she thought him rather dull—her own tastes were for rumbustious young men with big muscles and one-track minds—but now she was older and wiser and Simon's Harley Street world seemed to her like paradise lost. Of course she had kept in touch with Simon and never let him know of her disillusionment. She liked to think she had such a fine, influential friend, especially since he hadn't married anyone else and so could, presumably, still be in love with her memory.

'Why can't Howard see that it's over?' she asked herself fiercely. 'All that's left is the habit, the contempt of over-familiarity, and he can't understand that I'm bored when he's with me and bored when he's away. I'm bored, bored, *bored*!'

A steward-boy tapped on the veranda door and entered.

'Madame MacDon'l?' he queried.

'Yes? Well, what is it?' She always spoke arrogantly to servants. Nobody could tell her they were her equals, not in a thousand years.

'Please to come to office, Madame.'

'Damn!' she thought. 'It'll be Howard on the phone, of course, asking what the hell I think I'm doing. How dare his wife, his "possession", dare to run away and play by herself! Well, I'm just in the mood to tell him!'

Earl Farrant, the club secretary, looked anywhere but at her when she entered the main office, however. He was a big, blond, typical Canuck, and was only doing a job of this nature because he had lost an arm in a car accident. He spoke to his blotter.

'Siddown, Katie, will ya'—she hated being called Katie; Howard did it, and so of course did all his friends and acquaintances—'I'm afraid I've got bad news.'

She felt peculiarly faint, wondering what could be classed as bad news to one who was on the brink of so many possible disasters, to whom even the prospect of staying here for a further two and a half years was the worst possible news.

Earl went on uneasily, 'It's Howard. I'm afraid he——'

Katrina said calmly, 'You're not trying to tell me Howard's dead, are you?'

The secretary looked up at that. 'Yes, I am. The news just came through. They found his body in a ravine. His jeep had struck a boulder on a bend in the road. He was knocked dead cold, Katie. What I mean is it was instantaneous, I guess. He didn't suffer.'

She repeated, 'Knocked dead cold.' Earl hadn't meant to make a macabre joke and somehow it struck her as horribly funny. Dead cold, or cold dead, both were so applicable.

She began to laugh shrilly, her mouth a grimace and tears streaming from her eyes. Earl said 'Stop that!' quietly at first, and then yelled it so that she shuddered once or twice and was silent.

'I guess I know how y'feel,' he said, and handed her a stiff whisky though it was but two-thirty in the afternoon. 'We'll all do what we can to help, Katie. Y'know that.'

'Yes, I know. I'll have to think.'

Her first thought, as she turned to leave the office, was, 'I'm free! Suddenly I'm free!' She remembered to be glad that Howard hadn't suffered.

CHAPTER SEVEN

KATSUNGI, to Joanna Rivers' surprise, was a town. She
had imagined her new appointment would take her
into what she had always imagined was typical Africa,
that her home would be a bungalow in a bush clearing
and her patients living in nearby mud huts. Katsungi,
however, had wide main streets lined with white concrete supermarkets and department stores; true there
was the occasional small trader setting up his stall like
an unwelcome barnacle in the shadow of his more
well-to-do competitors, and behind the white façade of
shops there were some squalid and overcrowded little
streets, but it was all quite urban and therefore a little
disappointing to her.

The bungalow allotted to them, however, was
entirely to Joanna's liking. If she had been afraid
of having to cope without running water she was
now reassured. There were taps everywhere, and two
bathrooms, a shower-house and laundry-room. The
water was very good, and her only complaint was
that it was inclined to be turned off without warning. All this would be better, she was told, when the
new hydro-electric scheme was in full operation.

The living-room of the bungalow was large and airy
and a wide veranda led off it looking out over a well-
tended garden to a high hibiscus hedge which hid the
suburban road from view. The three bedrooms, however, were of the single variety and all contained a
small narrow bed, though comfortably sprung.

'This was bachelor accommodation previously,'
Simon ruefully explained. 'We do seem to have
the dickens of a job getting together, don't we,
dear?'

The furnishings were adequate though of a uniform
variety.

'We'll buy a decent carpet or two,' Simon decided, 'and you can have a blank cheque to purchase what a woman likes to have about the place.'

'Pretty curtains,' Joanna said promptly, 'are what this place needs.'

They were not to start work for a week, but they naturally wanted to see the people they were to relieve actually on the job. A Land-Rover had been placed at their disposal and they drove off to the new suburb of Nyerere, named after Tanzania's President, where streets of box-like houses stretched into infinity.

'These have been put up to house the workers on the project,' their guide, a medical orderly, told them. 'Unfortunately we can't build fast enough, and so we have a problem here——'

The 'problem' was a large area of no-man's-land verging on the bush where a squatter village of tents, mud huts and tin-can shanties had sprung up.

'No proper sanitation for all these people,' the guide proceeded, 'and so there is much sickness.'

Joanna was gazing in horror and pity at her first live child with a monstrous umbilical hernia. It walked awkwardly, at four or five years old, like a woman in advanced pregnancy.

'Oh, Simon!' she cried out. 'The poor little thing!'

In ten minutes she saw so many poor little things, and big ones, too, that she ceased to cry out, however. She wanted to start there and then to work her fingers to the bone for these, who would be her patients.

'Now we see more cheerful sight,' their guide pronounced, 'the community centre, hospital and clinic.'

The community centre contained a library, adult education lecture-rooms and a kindergarten.

'We try to teach mothers who have had no education how to read and write and care properly for their children,' the young man, whose name was Siegfried, though he was boot-polish black, explained. 'We also organise educational play-groups for the under-fives.

Unfortunately we then tend to lose touch with the children, for the Moslems like to run their own schools and most of the other schools are the Mission type. Many children fall between the two and are never educated outside of tribal folklore. We are trying to forge ahead, of course, and bring in a compulsory-education act. All takes time. Now this'—he pointed at a rather dilapidated-looking stucco building at which they had stopped—'is Katsungi General Hospital. It used to be outside the town, but as you see, town has grown very big. This'—he took them towards a small, bright, airy building—'is Madame Doctor's clinic, if you will pardon the expression?' Joanna, now looking more interested than ever, smiled acquiescently. 'It is your job, Madame, to treat patients and keep them from going'—he cocked his thumb at the hospital—'there. Hospital is now far too small for town's needs. Only serious cases admitted nowadays.'

They entered the clinic and Joanna was really impressed. There was no shortage of chromium and tile here and everything was clean, bright and shining. Here, too, it was Canadian money and enterprise which had provided the clinic. There were strong ties between Canada and Tanzania and Canadians were everywhere in large numbers.

Joanna met Doctor Maud Somers, herself a Canadian, who was soon to go home on well-deserved leave and return to private practice.

'Thought I'd see a bit of the world before I was too old,' she confessed chummily, 'and I have. More at times than I wanted to. Not that it's a bad place to work in; it isn't. But oh, lord, I wouldn't be born an African child if I could choose! There's still so much lying in wait which could either kill, blind or maim me for life, and if I had a fool of a mother into the bargain, who took me to a witch-doctor when I complained of earache, well then, just anything could happen.'

'Is there much ignorance?' Joanna asked.

'My dear, you're joking! Superstition still seethes here under the surface and will do for another hundred years or so. Families come in from the bush villages, lured by the chance of earning big money, and bring their ju-ju and voodoo with them. One backward family can quickly cause a dozen enlightened ones to retrogress back to paganism within a few weeks. A woman will dutifully bring her baby here for vaccination and immunisation and take him straight back to the witch-doctor (practising illegally, I may add) to have cow-dung put on his scabs for luck. I usually slap a few hundred units of penicillin into all injections that may cause an open sore. When one learns one's tropical medicine in the nice antiseptic atmosphere of a hospital, or training school, one should also learn about the black arts which were dealing with the problem before we came, and in some cases with success.'

'Doctor Somers, you're not serious!'

'I am. I've learned to respect certain aspects of witch-doctoring in my five years here. They know more about the human mind than we yet dream of. Try all your antibiotics, potions, ills and know-how on a healthy young woman with a septic finger who has been told by her witch-doctor that she will be dead within a week. I'm telling you now, she'll die. She'll be dying from the moment she's been told. I've seen it. It still goes on.'

Joanna shuddered. 'How horrible!'

'Still,' the other said comfortably, 'the old antibiotics still save the ninety and nine, so it's all worthwhile. This is my own personal timetable if you care to look it over. Maybe you'll want to change things. They haven't yet got the Pill here, so the ante-natal clinic takes up a whole day. They have their babies at home, of course, unless there are severe complications. This is a list of recognised midwives who have had partial training and can be guaranteed not to cut the umbilical cord with broken bottle-glass; previously a favourite method and responsible for most of the distended bellies you see about the place. You must see your mothers engage one of these ladies for the event, and if it's a new mum, drop in yourself, if possible, to show willing. Fortunately these people are not yet overbred and take rather better to motherhood than we whites. Then there's the baby-clinic and the E.N.T. and the Ophthalmic—got a lot of those, but Doctor Webber comes over from the hospital that day, so you just make a few helpful noises and do the drops. Dressings are done *every* day between eight and nine—got to in these temperatures—and house visits after siesta. Anything else?'

'Whew!' was Joanna's response to this.

'Oh, it'll come, my girl. And I can guarantee you'll never be bored for a moment.'

'I shouldn't think there'd be time,' Joanna agreed, smiling.

'Still, you've got your hubby. I lost mine in Korea. The damn' fool needn't have volunteered. . . .'

'I'm sorry. Need *you* have volunteered for this?'

'*Touchée!*' Doctor Somers laughed. 'No. When my son was newly qualified, he wanted to volunteer for Vietnam. Still, that's how it goes. One born every minute. Now, if you'll excuse me, Doctor, I must get on.'

Simon had been chatting all this while to the Hospital Director. He came across to Joanna as she stood by the Land-Rover.

'The hospital's rather awful,' he volunteered, 'they're all dying before they're admitted. Now when patients have to go into hospital for an operation they plead to be allowed home the following day or give themselves up for dead. There's a big new hospital being built farther out, but it won't be functioning for a year or two. How's the clinic?'

'Every mod. con., and Doctor Somers taught me more in ten minutes than I learned at the Nestor in a month. It should be very interesting, but I see myself like one of those Hindu gods, with about six pairs of arms.'

'If you grow more than your present slim two I shall protest. Now shall we go and see my department?'

They drove out to the site of the enterprise which had caused the present population explosion in Katsungi. A brown, sluggish river, the Katsungi, from which the town was named, ran between verdant banks of strange, tough, leather-leaved and often floriferous trees with exotic parasites attached to them. At present the river ran aimlessly, widening into mangrove swamps, and harbouring breeding grounds for pests, but the government was now putting the Katsungi River to work. They were building a man-made diversion for the waters which would trap them in a vast dam, providing both more tap water and cheap electricity. At present the man-made part of it looked rather like a lunar landscape, all dust and stones and ugliness. There were white men, brown men and black men scrambling about like ants, all wearing the regulation steel helmets and orange jackets provided for the job.

'And where'—Joanna asked politely—'do you come in all this?'

Simon made a playful pass at her chin and retorted, 'Well, not mixing concrete, I can assure you.'

They had left Siegfried behind at the clinic, but when they made themselves known at one of the huts on the site a ginger-haired, stocky young man came to meet them.

'Hiya, Doc! I'm Doc Whittle.'

Simon, who was tempted to reply Hiya in reply, said, 'How d'you do,' and held out his hand.

'I'm getting out while I'm still sane; you're relieving me, so I hear? Bossom's another year to go. He's already gone.'

'Gone?' Simon echoed, clambering after the other towards a long low white building overlooking the site.

'Round the bend,' Doctor Whittle explained succinctly. 'It gets us all in time. This is where we hang out and hold sick parades. Mostly we're involved in accidents on the site. They're bloody and regular—begging your pardon, ma'am—despite the most elaborate precautions. The b——' Doctor Whittle glanced again at Joanna and changed his epithet to—'silly asses will try to take naps on the job. Spent their life sleeping before they took to working for a living. Last week we had a gentleman went to bye-byes in a hole in the rubble tip. Got himself picked up by the grab and lost both legs.' Joanna felt a little sick. 'Things like that.' The young man shrugged. 'Happens all the time. We sewed up his stumps right here,' he nodded towards a room set up as a miniature operating theatre.

'Where is the fellow now?' Simon asked with interest.

'At home. Doctor Somers at the clinic shoves penicillin into him. He'll get a pair of artificial legs, of course. We have our own team providing aids.'

'It seems odd that you have so much and yet such an inadequate hospital.'

'We're building, but where are your nurses for a big hospital, eh, Doc? The girls we're sending home, and to the U.K. for training, will just be about ready to staff when we've finished the job. Our motto is keep 'em healthy. We hand out vitamins, provide the main meal of the day, examine every recruit before he signs on and refer the rejects to the proper authorities. Had a fellow with a collapsed nose-bridge tried to sign on only yesterday. "What happened to yer face, feller?" I asked. "Fight," he says. Knew he was lying. He was an active leper and simply wanted to get in on the big money. Told him to go to the leprosarium and he said he'd just come from there and tried to put a curse on me. That's the sort of thing we're up against or rather you are, Doc. I'm headin' home. Winnipeg, here I come!'

They had much to think and talk about that evening as they discussed the jobs which had now assumed the proportions of reality.

'Like to run home?' Simon asked as they sat side by

side in lounging chairs enjoying whisky macs and large, sweet local nuts.

'No. I'm going to do something about it.'

'So am I. Especially knowing I can always come home to you, Jo.'

It was the first time he had used the diminutive, and she thought of Nick breathing that name into her ear before he had defected to Yvonne. It made her go all stiff and feel peculiar so that though she knew Simon was all set for a love scene she failed to respond.

'Don't call me that, Simon,' she asked him.

'Oh, I'm sorry. You have a beautiful name, anyway, and I shouldn't be the one to mutilate it. Shall we turn in?'

He paused on the threshold of the room she had made hers and grimaced at the narrow bed with its mosquito-net tucked in all round.

'Remind me to go shopping for *married quarters*,' he said moodily, kissed her and went to his own room.

Possibly because she missed having him near she lay awake far into the night, viewing the size of the job she had undertaken to do and feeling pathetically inadequate to do it.

Joanna had never suspected that she could be so happy less than three months after the day she had imagined her heart to be shattered into fragments by one man's defection. She wanted to tell all unhappy lovers of her success; advise them to do as she had done and marry someone else with the determination to make a go of it. She couldn't think what normal lovers had that she didn't possess, unless it was those whispered words (often born of the moment) breathed into ears attuned by the night sounds of sleepy birds and rustling leaves and enchanted waters.

Of course marriage without courtship had its blind side, which she was discovering. Instead of knowing Simon inside out before becoming his wife, she had to get to know him afterwards, and there was so much to Simon that at times she felt she was married to a com-

plete stranger. The gentle, persuasive and excitng
lover she already knew; the clever, competent, impati-
ent-with-inefficiency physician she also knew, and
respected, but the creature who went into brown
studies for an hour at a time, his only link with the
outside world the pipe in his mouth, she didn't know
at all and found vaguely unsettling.

The first time he had gone all withdrawn like this
she had tried to contact him.

'Simon, what shall we talk about? Our work? Or
shall we discuss culture? I don't know what we do
about culture here. There's no theatre or art gallery
and I don't hear much edifying conversation at the
clinic. I suppose one is inclined to vegetate if one
doesn't watch out. Everything was such a rush that I
only brought a couple of paperback novels with me
and I finished those ages ago. I can't read a book over
and over like some people do. If I know what's going
to happen——' She stopped speaking as she saw that
his eyes were not only upon her but also gleaming
strangely.

'Joanna,' he said, 'you're twittering like a parakeet.
Shut up, dear. I want to think.'

It was any casual exchange between any husband
and wife, and yet she was hurt and annoyed. To be
accused of 'twittering', indeed! On that occasion she had
taken her wounded feelings off to bed, but if she had
imagined Simon would notice and follow her to apologise, she was mistaken. She didn't hear a sound from
him for over an hour, while she lay stiff and expectant,
and when he came to her door she didn't reply to his
whispered 'Joanna?' and so for the first time in weeks
she went to sleep eventually without a goodnight kiss.

In the morning, over breakfast, he had been normally chatty and pleasant. She had a desire to bring
him up short with, 'Now you're twittering, Simon,
and *I* want to think,' but she managed to resist and
was glad, for retaliation is only for the small-minded.

It was obvious that some of her 'twitterings' had
registered, however, for he observed, 'If you want

something to read I have a case of books with me, not yet unpacked, but you're welcome to rummage any time. They're mostly travel and biographies, but I joined a book-club before leaving London, so we should have two works of fiction arriving monthly, once they start. It isn't quite the back of beyond, you know. The mail-man does get through.'

Another facet of his character she was doomed to discover was his anger, and this, though rarely aroused, was peculiarly Latin, hot, searing, and quickly burnt out.

He had told her seriously one evening, over dinner, 'Joanna, one of the engineers' wives was attacked last night. She's in a bad way, and quite hysterical.'

'Oh, dear!' She was genuinely distressed. 'Who was it? Have they caught him?'

'No. She can't say for sure who it was. It happened in the dark, in the bush. All she knows is that he was coloured. All Africans are inclined to look alike at night. Joanna,' he went on, 'until the cars arrive I don't want you to walk home from the clinic any more. Wait until I collect you in the jeep. Understand?'

'Oh, Simon, that's too absurd! It's only ten minutes' walk and I like to get home ahead of you to see that Maussa is cooking the dinner to our liking. I don't have to walk through bush, it's streets all the way.'

'Joanna, I want you to *wait for me*. The blasted dinner can wait for a bit. Now do you hear me?'

His frown was utterly masterful, so she smiled and said, 'They'll hear you back at St. Paul's if you shout like that! All right, if it will make you any happier I'll hang on at the clinic for you.'

For the next few nights she waited dutifully enough, always glad to see the jeep come round a bend in the road, however, with Simon at the wheel dressed in bush shirt and shorts, his usual working attire. One Thursday evening she finished very early. It had been the opthalmic clinic day and she had acted as Doctor Webber's assistant after the usual dressing round in the morning. The clinic was supposed to close between one and four in the afternoon, as the shops did, but Joanna did not take to the idea of having an afternoon siesta and then visiting her bedridden patients in the early evening. She preferred to work all afternoon and finish half an hour before Simon. She had no seriously ill patients at the moment, however, and so on this day she was finished by four o'clock. Two pregnancies were due to come to term any time, but as they were first babies they could overrun by as much as a week and the midwives engaged on the cases knew where she lived if she was needed. She surveyed the golden afternoon, hot and yet not blistering, and decided it would be lovely to go home and have a refreshing cup of tea in the garden before giving orders for dinner. It was broad daylight, too, and there were plenty of people about.

She left a note for Simon with the watchman, who cleaned the place and stayed on guard all night.

'Finished early. Gone home. Joanna.'

She had wanted to put 'Dear Simon', and end 'with love', but she feared her husband would not care to have endearments splashed about.

She didn't hurry as she walked, for there was plenty of time. She pondered that, after three weeks, she had slipped into the routine of the clinic very well. She was popular with her assistants, Siegfried, the orderly, and Nurse Sabiya. She had been called into the hospital once or twice to give her expert opinion on patients with cardiac troubles.

'Well, my husband is the true expert,' she had told the staff, touched, nevertheless, 'I was his registrar at St Paul's.'

Everyone was amazed that a consultant physician from London was now working on an African engineering project.

'He had his reasons,' Joanna smiled.

'He must have had, by golly!' was the rejoinder.

She was passing a narrow street which led to a

native bazaar in the distance and it looked colourful and attractive. One had to get behind the façade of the new to find the old. She turned into the narrow street and was immediately conscious of being a foreigner as she was the cynosure of curious, inexpressive and hostile dark eyes. Women outside the peeling adobe houses stopped gossiping to watch her progress; a child pointed and then ducked behind its mother's skirts; as she was smiling at another toddler its mother, again pregnant, waddled forward and swept it from her path; two young men regarded her with insolent contempt and one tried to imitate her walk, much to the other's delight.

She got much the same sort of treatment in the bazaar. Here she was a stranger and a not particularly welcome one. There wasn't another white face to be seen. She examined the stalls, feeling uncomfortable that her presence brought down a curtain of silence. One child at her heels collected another and then another until she felt like the Pied Piper heading her column away from their homes and loved ones. They were not begging either. When she held out a small coin the nearest child ignored it and merely stared up at her sullenly.

She was sorry now that she had come. She was intruding and was being told so in mime. The Europeans did their marketing in Main Street and Independence Square; they were expected to keep to their own herd; the buffalo does not stray into the ranks of the zebra, or the lion rub noses with the leopard.

She felt a sharp, wounding blow on the back of her leg and knew a pebble had been thrown. She turned and a woman was cuffing her small son, obviously chiding him for the act, but when Joanna looked around her she saw a stone cast at her in every eye and knew it was time to go back the way she had come, the illusion of enchantment for ever gone from that particular scene.

It was then a bunch of women began to cry out and scatter in all directions. Down a narrow alleyway between the stalls staggered a youth of about sixteen; his eyes were rolling and a grey saliva dribbled from the corners of his thick lips. He looked as though he was trying to find something to cling to, and then with a little gurgle of despair fell prone into the dust, jerked once or twice and was still.

Nobody approached him, but one or two women pointed and said the Swahili word for 'Devil', with which Joanna was becoming accustomed.

Somebody screamed as she ran forward and turned the boy on his back. Only the whites of his eyes showed and the dribble from his lips was thicker than ever. His breath hissed through the congestion of spittle and she fished in the light medical bag she always carried and sought a spatula which she rammed, with difficulty, between his teeth and fished at the tongue which was curling back to choke the lad. Having got the tongue under control and wiped out his mouth she turned his head to one side and waited for him to come out of the fit. A few women had crept a little nearer, but still fearfully. As the lad sighed and his eyes opened Joanna injected him and he rubbed his thigh ruefully, now beginning to smile. He looked like any normal boy by now. The audience sighed, 'Whyee!'

'Does anybody here speak English?' Joanna asked.

There was no answer for a minute, and then a young boy edged sheepishly forward, propelled by his mother.

'I speak good English,' he said modestly, 'also Swahili and *das ist gut* in German.'

'Very clever,' said Joanna. 'Do you know this boy?'

'Yes. His name is Kito. Devils live in him, as you have seen.'

'What's your name, boy?'

'Julius, after our President.'

'Well, Julius, anybody who knows two languages and *das ist gut* in German doesn't really believe that devils live in people. I'm a doctor and this boy is an epileptic. That is he has fits. It's a disease, like yaws or hookworm, nothing to do with devils.'

The boy looked uncertain and his mother was obviously asking, 'What's she saying? What's she saying?'

'I want you to tell this boy's mother and father that he should come to the clinic for treatment. We can help him.'

Julius told this to his mother, who looked amazed and then broke into a flow of words.

'My mother says she will tell Kito's parents what you say, but that there are many devils in people which she has seen with her own eyes. She says devils like to live in our country and white people don't really know about them.'

'Well, please tell your mother I'm interested in all she says, but that I know I can help Kito. I haven't been in your country very long, but I like working here and hope to make many friends.'

The atmosphere was noticeably easier after that and one young woman came forward who had actually received treatment for an abscess at the clinic under Joanna. She was obviously telling all her friends of the relief when the abscess had been incised, and a committee of welcome then escorted the young doctor from stall to stall. She wanted to buy Simon a present, something quite personal, and thought he might like an ebony pipe-rack with carved animal heads. It cost the equivalent of twenty-five shillings, and then the sun was getting dangerously low in the sky and so she waved goodbye to her new-found friends and turned for home. She didn't fancy going down the narrow street again, in the dusk, with those insolent young men mincing after her, so she tried another way and became hopelessly lost. By the time she had extricated herself it was quite dark, for twilight is an elusive fairy in the tropics, who reveals herself for only a moment in the day.

She thought her watch must be fast, for it read half past six as she arrived home without further incident.

'Simon!' she called as she passed the living-room. 'Sorry I'm late, I——'

There was no one in the house, she saw with surprise, neither Simon nor the servants who were composed of Maussa, the cook, Richard, who cleaned and waited at table and Small-boy, who was always called that and helped Maussa and ran errands.

She turned, puzzled, to hear the jeep roar up to the front door with Simon in it, his face distorted and strange.

'Simon?' she greeted him questioningly.

He stopped and looked up at her. His voice came at her flatly.

'Are you all right?'

'Me? I'm all right. Where *is* everyone. I'm sorry I'm late, but——'

He was up the steps in a bound and upon her like an enraged bull. His hands gripped her shoulders in a vice and he shook until her teeth rattled in her skull. Her gift to him flew out of her hands and broke in two on the cement floor.

'I don't care what the hell you've been doing, only that you failed to do as you were told!' he roared. 'I've been scouring the damned streets looking for you for more than an hour wondering what horrible thing I was going to find or be told! I have the boys out in all directions searching! I was just going to phone the police, hoping I wasn't being a fool, and you have the audacity to ask where *is* everyone!'

He appeared to realise what he was doing and the twin flames in his eyes died out as he released her. She felt like a rag doll dropped by a playful puppy, all limp and boneless.

'I'm sorry,' he told her, as she staggered to a chair. 'I suppose I was hurting you. I've never laid a finger on a woman before. I can only repeat that I'm sorry.'

'That's all right, Simon. I'm sorry for causing you anxiety. I didn't mean to.'

They both needed a breathing space and he now sat opposite her, looking strangely pale beneath his suntan. He eventually tried to break the ice, or rather, bridge the red-hot lava flowing between them by making a heavy joke.

'So now you can tell all your friends your husband beats you, Joanna.'

'No, I won't do that,' she felt her face crack as she smiled, 'and it wasn't a beating. I think I understand——'

'I wonder if you do. That woman the other day—remember I examined her, or rather, I examined you. It was you I saw, Joanna, bruised and torn, as it would be if ever——' He shuddered, and she laid a trembling hand on his knee.

'Simon, I know you had a terrible shock when that happened, but one can't live one's life in fear because of one disaster. When I was small there was something of the sort happened in our district and my mother refused to let me out. Of course that couldn't go on indefinitely, and we had to learn to carry on as usual after I'd been warned not to speak to strangers, all the obvious precautions. I'm sorry, but I can't live my life in constant fear here, either. I can't wait about for you to escort me as though I'm a half-wit. I'm a grown woman, and I may remind you I'm also a doctor. I could give a pretty good account of myself if I was attacked, and I'll carry an old surgical knife with me if it would make you feel any better. But don't let us get things out of proportion. There's quite a large white community here and only one woman has been assaulted.'

'Oh, Joanna!' He suddenly held her to him, his hands as fevered in their caresses as they had been fierce in anger. 'You must be black and blue. I'm sorry. My mother used to say I don't have a temper, I have periodic eruptions. May I'—his voice dropped persuasively—'come and see you into bed and kiss every bruise better?'

'Of course.' They parted hastily as the first of the boys returned. It was Maussa, looking most happy to see his mistress safe and well.

'I open can,' he announced. 'No time cook now.'

'Soup and an omelette will be fine, Maussa,' Joanna told him.

Funnily enough she felt closer to Simon in those hours after his angry outburst than she had done since their arrival in Africa. He even said he would stick the pipe-rack together because it was the first thing she had given him and he would treasure it for ever.

After he had kissed all her bruises better, however, he had to leave her, grumbling over the delay of the local furniture store to produce a bed suitable for married folk's needs.

CHAPTER EIGHT

THE Saturday following the day when Joanna recorded in her diary that she had now been married seven weeks proved to be a notable day indeed. For the first time during her stay in Katsungi she awoke feeling unwell, both sick and dizzy, and lurched to the bathroom to vomit. She wondered if she was starting a malarial attack, though she was particular about using a mosquito net, even while hating it, and also took paludrin regularly. Just as she was considering asking Simon to take her temperature and give his professional opinion, however, she suddenly felt better and even hungry, so she showered and dressed, meeting Simon on the veranda for breakfast without mentioning her earlier malaise.

There was no return of the unpleasant symptoms all day and during the afternoon as she dozed in a lounging chair and Simon tackled a week-old *Times* crossword puzzle, there was great excitement from the boys' quarters and Richard burst on to the veranda.

'Sir! Madame! Men here with two motorcars. Say for you.'

Outside in the road was quite a motorcade, with Simon's Jaguar recognisable under a coat of red dust; next was Joanna's wedding present and wish, her own blue Sunbeam Rapier, again covered in dust, and lastly a very old claptrap of all sorts, like a mongrel dog, which was apparently the delivery boys' transport back to Mombasa. Simon had arranged for the vehicles to be delivered rather than take time off from his new job to go and collect them.

There was, of course, much haranguing and bargaining over payment for the service, which started off by being three times what had been arranged with the garage owner on the docks at Mombasa, at which Simon had called after disembarking from the *Chieftain*, and handing over the various documents. Richard, who was inclined to be hot-blooded and extremely suspicious of the citizens of all neighbouring African states, was all for starting a fight with the greedy Kenyans. Simon told him to cool down, however, and the drivers eventually handed over the ignition keys, took their money and a couple of tins of English cigarettes and went off in the jalopy for the long journey back to Mombasa.

Joanna said she wanted to try her car out.

'I don't think we got you a Tanzanian licence,' Simon demurred, 'and I don't even know whether you can drive or not.'

'I can,' Joanna put out her tongue at him. 'If you get in with me can I just cruise to the end of the road and back?'

Simon was scrambling into the passenger when Richard again stuck his oar in.

'I cannot allow my master and madame to ride in such a *dirty* car,' he said severely. 'Peoples will think you have very lazy boys.'

'Just five minutes,' Joanna promised, 'then you can have it.'

Simon said as they moved away from the open ditch at the roadside, 'Like it?'

'Oh, Simon, I haven't words.'

'I want you to be happy, Joanna. Are you?'

'Very happy. And—Simon?'

'Yes?'

'It didn't take this, you know. I was happy without my car. It will just be an added pleasure.'

He looked at her hungrily.

'Let's go and change into the Jag and go and see if our bed has arrived in the store yet!'

Needles of awareness shot through her as she felt his masculine need reach out and embrace her.

The store manager said he was very sorry, but it was such a special bed and had to come from Dar-es-Salaam. As soon as it arrived it would be delivered and his men would set it up complete with mattress.

'The way we've nagged about this bed,' Joanna joked, 'must be quite a talking point in the store.'

'Oh, I hadn't thought I might appear ridiculous. I'm sorry, Joanna.'

'Oh, no! I didn't mean. . . .' But she realised she had offended no matter what her intention. The very nature of their relationship was so tenuous that it needed what they had found together on the ship to keep it functional. They were beginning to forget one another and now, by reason of her thoughtless remark, Simon felt snubbed. Instead of a man expressing normal desire for his mate, she had made him feel like a deprived animal, howling in abandon at the moon.

Again she learned something about her husband, that it was easier to drive him away than to hold him. He was like slippery elm all evening, shooting off about business of his own, writing up reports and setting out his books, works of fiction on some shelves and medical and surgical textbooks on others, all neatly listed in alphabetical order.

She grew tired of following him about, her offers of help being politely rejected. When the boys had finished their duties and gone off to their quarters she decided to have things out with him.

'Simon,' she began nervously; he had decided to go back to his crossword, 'you asked me this afternoon if I was happy and I said I was, that it didn't take cars and things like that'—he looked up at her, his expression an enigma—'well,' she told him, 'I'm not very happy at this moment. I don't understand your mood.'

'I wasn't aware——' he began coldly, and then decided to shame the devil. 'I don't understand it myself,' he said frankly. 'There are so many first times in this business. For the first time this afternoon I saw myself through your eyes as a rutting stag. I was annoyed and—and ashamed. You see, I'm not like that. You made me feel self-conscious.'

'I know, and I didn't mean to. I'm sorry. You must understand that I'm self-conscious, too. Such a little while ago I looked up to you as my boss only, and yet here I am sharing a house with you and waiting, not very patiently, to share a double bed. I'm sometimes confused by the wonder of it all and make stupid observations to hide my real feelings. Coming out of that store today I felt overwhelmed by all the implications of this bed we've ordered; it's five feet six wide and has a criss-cross base allowing air to reach the mattress, and there'll be room for both of us all the time. No wonder I said the first silly thing which came into my head and groaned to myself when I felt you shy off as you did.'

He said, 'Well, Joanna, thanks for clearing the air. These are early days; days of probation for both of us. Can you see us graduating into old and experienced marrieds eventually? Perhaps growing alike as we totter along for our pensions together?'

'Why not?' she smiled.

'Let's go for a walk,' he suggested. 'It's hot indoors.'

The night was sticky, but it was cooler down by the river and though the mosquitoes were persistent in their buzzing they didn't care for the insect-repellent soap these white folk used so liberally. The moon sailed up out of the Indian ocean and brought its own magic along; its green-white light made even the brown river look like liquid silver and nocturnal flowers opened their cups and breathed perfume into the night.

At first Simon and Joanna held hands as they walked, and then there was a desire to be even closer and arms circled each other so that every step created the harmony found in a heart-searing prelude. It was Joanna who stopped and spoke, and Simon, a little dazed, thought she said, 'Who needs a bed!'

When he took her in his arms and felt her response he was in complete agreement with her sentiments; the moss was soft and damp beneath them and it was impossible to feel self-conscious in those surroundings under that tropic melon moon.

The prelude had been sweet, but the fugue was even sweeter.

The night watchman at the bungalow, who had been sneaking his usual nap in the most lifeless of night's hours, rubbed sleep from his eyes in amazement as his employers wandered home hand in hand, singing softly, at two o'clock in the morning.

By the following Wednesday a rather startling rhythm was obvious in Joanna's days. The boy, Richard, awoke her at six-thirty with a cup of tea, but as she sat up to drink she was overcome by a violent nausea and lurched to the bathroom feeling really awful. Within fifteen minutes, however, she was as well as ever, sometimes even better than ever, feeling vigorous and alive and ready for whatever the day would bring.

On this day, having had her now usual early morning experience, she sat down to breakfast, avoiding Simon's eyes because she fancied her own were too revealing.

'Good morning, my dear wife!'

'Morning!' she murmured into her coffee.

'Oh, do I detect a slight liverishness? Too many sundowners,' he teased her. They usually enjoyed a couple of whisky-sodas or brandy-ginger ales in the evenings together.

'No liver,' she told him, and her eyes ricocheted off his. 'I must rush. Busy day,' she said.

'Yes.' He was obviously puzzled by her attitude and fancied she didn't want to chat. Usually he left half an hour before she did, but he deliberately dallied, thinking she might not be well. He didn't know about the bathroom sessions.

She finally said, 'Aren't you late?' and went out to her car without raising her face to be kissed.

He thought, 'So this is one of *her* moods. I hope they don't happen too often,' and passed her on the road in his more powerful Jag with the most casual of salutes.

It was the day Joanna held her clinic for new patients and a long column of dark humanity was already weaved round the compound outside the clinic building; mothers with lethargic children hanging round their knees and babes with sore eyes and thin, sickly wails, old men and women with loose wrinkled skin hanging in empty folds and a few languid young adults with various complaints.

Every day more and more families arrived looking for work, mainly agriculturists whose crops had failed due to drought. There was nowhere for them to go, so they 'squatted', adding to the problems already existing and risking the pestilences their habits invited.

Joanna deliberately forbade herself the luxury of her own private thoughts until later. Siegfried, immaculate in clean white shirt and shorts, his cap jaunty upon his stubble hair, was out marshalling the crowds, bringing those actually suffering pain to the fore for early attention. He then sat at the table in the corner, a large pile of blank treatment cards at the ready, prepared to act as interpreter and liaison officer betweeen doctor and patient. Nurse Sabiya had prepared her dressing trolley and was boiling the instruments in the autoclave; often the hospital instruments came over for similar treatment, their autoclave being more often out of action than not.

Joanna signalled that all was ready when she perceived the instruments laid out between sterile towels, and the first patient was brought in.

The pathetic, weary toddler, sick to within inches of its life, one side of its head so swollen that the ear was sunk into it, told its own story before the young doctor could lay a finger on it. Mastoidal infections were very common in these parts. She gave the poor little thing a shot of morphia, tied a pink card round its neck and sent it, with its mother and Nurse Sabiya, across to the hospital for immediate operation, phoning her colleagues in the building to expect the visitors. She now knew the ritual. After the child had spent a few hours in the recovery-room, after the operation, it would be taken home and nursed there with herself in attendance twice a day.

The next patient was a young mother with mastitis. The affected breast was tightly swollen and very painful. Joanna drained it of milk and then injected the girl—she was only about nineteen—with several thousand units of penicillin and told her only to feed her baby at the unaffected side for several days. Armed with penicillin cream for outward use, the mother went off quite happily and the next patient was admitted, an old woman with a lighter skin than the majority of locals and heavily wrapped up in black draperies.

There was a curtained cubicle in one corner with an examination couch, and it was here that Joanna examined her orthodox Moslem women away from Siegfried's sight. The old woman toddled behind these obediently and shouted her symptoms so that the lad could interpret as she removed her rather smelly draperies. It was a case of pain in the abdomen increasing as the weeks went by. Joanna's heart sank as she heard this, for she was almost convinced by the crone's age and appearance that it was cancer eating away at her vitals.

All that was to be done in a case of this sort was numb the pain, make the time remaining more endurable. Taking the old woman's name and address, Joanna promised she would visit her again in the evening; that she was to come to the clinic every day at nine and await the doctor's call later in the day. The drug was already taking effect and the old woman expressed her thanks profusely and said she was glad now that she had come to see the *hakym*. This Arabic word convinced Joanna that before her was a descendant of settlers from Arabia, who were to be found in great numbers, chiefly on the coast.

Joanna dealt with toothaches, boils and abscesses; diagnosed an early case of bilharzia, several malarias and an elephantiasis, removed a toe-nail and a large splinter under local anesthetics, plucked out a fishbone lying embedded in the soft palate of one sufferer and sent a handless man to the leprosarium in a different part of the town for treatment. An entire family, coughing and emaciated, she directed across to the hospital for X-rays, and then Siegfried announced that she could now take her coffee break. The daily dressing round came next and she felt in need of ten minutes' complete relaxation before starting another phase of work.

She liked to have her coffee outside where she could watch the world go by, and her favourite spot was under a weird old baobab, that clown among trees which looks as though it has grown upside down and has roots where others have branches: there is a native story that such is the case. The Creator was so disgusted when He saw the first baobab that he tried it the other way up and found the result an improvement, ludicrous as it might be. A few vestigial leaves hanging here and there proved that the baobab knew what it was doing, however, and since Joanna's arrival it had sprouted a gaudy bouquet of the most exotic-looking flowers, in which ants were busy for most of the day.

Still she could not bring herself to think about herself and what must be faced. She welcomed the distraction accorded by a small procession walking down the street comprised of three very tall, handsome young men and an equally tall girl. They must all have topped six foot and the tallest would easily be six foot seven. The men were not overdressed, being clad in minute loin-cloths and long capes. The girl wore a kind of sarong, belted with beads at the middle. The strangers were handsome to a degree, living carvings of glorious, natural life and vigour.

'Siegfried!' Joanna called. 'Who are those people?'

The orderly looked contemptuous and grimaced.

'Masai,' he said, frowning. 'Very ignorant people who only know about cattle. They refuse to be educated. Such people hold our country back from progress.'

'But they look very healthy,' Joanna protested. 'Maybe their life agrees with them.'

'Not with us,' Siegfried said shortly. 'They are a problem.'

'But so beautiful and so natural,' Joanna continued to herself, 'like a pride of lions. Marvellous teeth, clear skins, the best specimens I've seen since I came here. They *are* life.'

And I'm life, she at last admitted, which is why I recognised them. I'm pregnant and there it is. How is it I, a qualified M.D., didn't recognise the symptoms of creation in my own self? I told Simon on the ship that I wasn't—couldn't be. What did I expect? A peal of bells or an attack of the vapours? Simon's child is here in me and I should be happy, but how can I be with all the confusion it's going to cause me—him—everybody? I can only carry on here so long, and I think some people are going to be very annoyed. And what will Simon say? Will he welcome it? Won't he feel, as I do, rushed into parenthood before he's ready for it? We're not really adjusted to living together yet. I don't know how to tell him. I think I'll wait another month and then I'll be absolutely sure one way or the other.

When Joanna arrived home exhausted after twenty-five visits that same day, she was greeted by Richard evincing great excitement. At such times his English was inclined to slip into pidgin.

'Madame! Kettle him not boilum for tea yet. Come look! Come look! Such a t'ing I long time no see.'

She followed him into the largest bedroom which she had used so far exclusively. The narrow bed had vanished and in its place was the large one she and Simon had chosen from a catalogue. It was a divan type with an extended sapele headboard having a most beautiful grain, polished into a gold mirror. There were two plump pillows, not yet sweat-stained, fine lawn sheets and a brocade bedspread. It all looked very nice, and yet Joanna's heart sank unaccountably.

Simon arrived and was also brought in to see the miracle.

'Well, there it is at last.' Simon's hand crept round

his wife's shoulders. He gave her a little squeeze as Richard ran to the screaming kettle in the kitchen. Maussa was a serious cook and did not consider making tea one of his duties.

'Now there's plenty of bed, but hardly any room,' Joanna joked heavily.

Simon said, 'Are you very tired?'

'I'll say I am. But I suppose you are, too.' She sat on the bed wondering how she could keep those morning sessions from Simon if they were to sleep together. Normally he used the shower-house while she had use of the bathroom. Thus she had complete privacy while she was feeling nauseated.

Simon took the tea-tray from Richard and handed her a cup while he lounged against the dressing-table fiddling with her toiletries.

'Joanna, a few days ago you accused me of having a mood. Today I sense one in you. Is it because of anything I've done?'

She half laughed and wanted to say, 'And how!' Instead she said, 'No, nothing like that. Wednesday's always a bit much. Let's put it down to that.'

'You do seem very tired today. I hope this job isn't going to prove too tough for you. After all, you're tackling a new climate as well. Answer frankly if you'd rather I didn't sleep here tonight.'

Almost too readily her reply came, 'Well, if you wouldn't mind . . .'

'Not at all.' He bowed smilingly and they might have been either side of a wide river in a matter of moments.

'I may have a confinement tonight,' she tried to explain. 'If so, I wouldn't wish to disturb you. You do understand?'

Across an arctic waste his voice assured her that he did. She wondered whether or not to blurt her secret out there and then, but the opportunity passed as he disappeared to shower and change.

Although familiarity is said to breed contempt, Joanna would have given anything to be familiar with this husband of hers and understand how to approach him. He was obviously trying to keep a sociability between them on this evening so that he could not be accused of throwing a mood, but they were in different dimensions. She remembered how, as her superior and mentor back at St Paul's, he had always pounced on any half-truth or incomplete fact, and now it seemed obvious to her that he was aware her possible confinement was the excuse hiding her true reason for not wanting him with her and he was too proud to challenge her.

They played bezique and had a game of chess, though she really couldn't give him a game. He beat her playing without his queen quite easily.

In that great bed, alone, it was ages before Joanna slept. She was aware not only of her condition but also of a deepening regard for the man who was her husband. Now she couldn't image life without him and yet fancied he felt nothing for her outside of the physical, which he hadn't felt all along throughout their acquaintance.

Next day she had determined not to allow misunderstanding to build up between them like a wall but to confide her suspicions about her condition to the one other person who had a right to know. When she rose, however, had her bad ten minutes and then arrived on the veranda ready and eager for breakfast, there was only a note awaiting her under the marmalade pot.

REPORTING IN EARLY. BOSSOM HAVING A MALARIAL ATTACK. SEE YOU THIS EVENING. SIMON.

Joanna could have wept, childishly, from disappointment, and Richard didn't make her feel any better when he observed, 'Why master no sleep in new bed? In my country a wife always sleep with husband.'

'Don't be impertinent!' Joanna scolded him. 'What we do isn't your business.'

She felt mean as she saw his crestfallen expression,

and this steeled her determination to confide in Simon as soon as possible. A coming child should bind a household closer together, not cause quarrels and misunderstandings. She felt happier all day for her decision and couldn't get home quickly enough. She soothed Richard by complimenting him on the spick and span appearance of the house and then jollied Maussa into preparing his most successful dish, chicken curry with a dozen or so trimmings and snowy rice. Simon was very fond of curry and she wanted all to go particularly well this evening.

A great deal of mail, including much from overseas, had arrived and Joanna settled clown to read a long letter from her mother.

'Yvonne and that Nick of hers—yours—whoever he does belong to, have had a terrible row and now she says she wouldn't marry him if he was the last man on earth. I can't help worrying about that girl, and it would be nice to have her married and someone else's responsibility. She complains that Nick keeps comparing her with you, to her detriment, and she's beginning to hate the sound of your name, which is a terrible thing for a sister to say. Tanzania sounds terrible—so hot. I don't think I could stand the heat. Watch out you don't get wrinkled as some people do in the tropics. Always wear a hat. . . .'

There was much more in a similar vein; Tessa Frear didn't write memorable letters. They managed to sound exactly like her voice, whining and complaining.

There were other letters from various friends of medical school days, all writing in response to Joanna's big news, that she was now married.

When she heard Simon drive up she dropped the lot, however, her heart pounding with excitement. As she kissed him she pressed hard and his eyes questioned hers as she drew away.

'Had a better day?' he asked, conversationally.

'Yes. Simon, I—I have something to tell you. Drink?'

'Please. Ah, I see we have some mail. Would it wait until I see if there's anything important?'

'Of course.' She poured him a sherry and handed it to him as he sat at the desk reading his mail. She sat on the edge of the bamboo chaise-longue expectantly. His back was very broad and his head so dark and handsome. She found herself wondering what the baby would look like and hoped it favoured Simon no matter what its sex. She couldn't think of it as a child in her arms, but could see a schoolboy edition of Simon quite clearly in her mind's eye. He had a dark roguish eye and thick black hair.

Her vision came from within to regard her husband again. He hadn't moved. He appeared to be rigid and then she heard him murmuring over and over again, 'Oh, my God! Oh, how awful! Oh, God!'

'Simon, is anything wrong?' she asked him.

He turned and looked at her without seeing her. She had never seen him so unaware of her since their marriage; he had been annoyed and angry with her, but never unconscious of her presence. He spoke like one in a bad dream.

'Poor Katrina! How can I reach her? How in God's name can I help?'

In growing panic Joanna began to batter at his chest.

'Simon, this isn't fair! Tell me what's happened? Tell me!'

At last he became conscious of what she was doing.

'Please don't do that!' He spoke in some irritation. 'I've had bad news.'

'I gathered that,' she almost snapped. 'Now tell me.'

'Katrina MacDonald, my—er—friend in the south, lost her husband in a dreadful accident. The awful part is that she wrote me asking for help and comfort, and of course I hadn't told her I was coming out here myself. The letter went to London and was re-addressed to me here. The accident happened eight weeks ago. Poor Katrina must be concluding that she turned in her grief the wrong way.'

Joanna had a thought which stuck in her like a dagger. Eight weeks ago Simon wasn't quite married to me. If she had cabled she might have changed history. Aloud she said, 'There's the telephone for what it's worth. Would she be on the phone?'

He glanced again at the letter still in his hand.

'She's staying at some club. The Canuck Club, Dar-es-Salaam 3610. I suppose our damned phone is still out of order?'

'I haven't tried it today.' She proceeded to do so. 'As dead as the dodo,' she said. 'There's a phone in the Imperial hotel down the road.'

'Right. See you later,' he tossed at her, and was gone in a flash. She heard the Jag roar away.

'My big news rather died stillborn in all that,' she told the empty room. She felt hurt and rebuffed. Reason told her that Simon would want to be a friend in need, a prop to stay the hurt and bereaved no matter who they were. His behaviour was natural and founted from a kindly heart. Her news would keep until a more propitious moment.

Maussa came in from the kitchen to announce that the dinner was ready, the rice was as Master liked it.

'Try to keep it going, Maussa, a bit longer. Master has gone to telephone.'

It was more than an hour before Simon returned, however, and his brow was like thunder.

'Forty damned minutes it took to get through,' he almost seethed, 'and then three hundred parakeets using the same blasted line!' She had never heard him so exasperated before in their acquaintance. 'However, I did manage to make myself understood. Katrina was suprised to know I was here and—and married. . . .'

He gave an odd little laugh and again the dagger plunged into Joanna's heart. He looked oddly embarrassed as he proceeded, 'Katrina was in a bit of a flat spin, naturally. She wants to stay out here until her affairs are settled, pension arranged and so forth. She hasn't been back to the house except to collect her things and she's rather tired of life at the club; the other members are obviously wearing carpet-slippers in her company, that sort of thing. So I—I asked her to come here. I hope that's all right with you?'

Though the night was sticky with heat, the fans stirring into a warm gale the still, hot air, Joanna shuddered unaccountably.

'This is your house,' she said in a thin, high voice, 'and you must do as you think best.'

'Well,' he said, 'I thought you would want to help too.'

'Of course,' she said. 'I take it you are Mrs Mac-Donald's only friend?'

'I don't understand you, Joanna. Are you being sarcastic?'

'No, I don't think so. I was simply thinking that with three hundred parakeets on the line you managed everything very well.'

'I think if it's going to cause unpleasantness, Joanna, Katrina had better stay at the Imperial.'

'Now don't be silly. She would presume I had raised objections in that case. I may not relish the idea of your old sweetheart in my house, but I'm not without sympathy.'

'I resent your reference to Katrina being my old sweetheart,' he said fiercely. 'Do you think I asked her here to——'

'Look, Simon, don't let's quarrel about it,' she said with sudden weariness. 'I'm sorry. I'm being small-minded and mean. I think you would understand why if you knew——' She glanced up at him and away again. How could she tell him she now had a greater claim on him than anyone else? Half of his mind, maybe more, was still on that telephone line to a club in Dar-es-Salaam. 'I'm sorry I didn't rise graciously, as expected. Now, what about dinner?'

'Actually I'm not hungry. This heat——'

'Oh. Maussa took great pains.'

'I'll tell him if you like. What about you?'

'I shall have my dinner, of course.'

'Do you mind if I look at the rest of my mail?'

'Of course not.'

How polite they were being! How proper!

When eventually they said goodnight they were not even trying to undo the damage caused that evening. They were not people who kissed out of habit, so they didn't attempt to kiss, and by tacit agreement Joanna once more found herself alone in the big bed which she was beginning to hate because it emphasised her aloneness. Also she was now haunted by grim possibilities. Simon had admitted to being once normally in love, that he had lost and suffered. He had always kept in touch with Katrina. Why? Unless he couldn't bear the idea of a complete severance. He had married her, Joanna, in a kind of hopeful arrangement, not knowing that his first and only love was now a widow and engaged in sending out an appeal for help and comfort. Would he have gone ahead with the 'arrangement' if he had known what he now knew? Was he at this moment calling himself every kind of a fool? She didn't know him enough to be able to read his mind. Funny how close one could be in the flesh to someone and yet never achieve the intimacy that is of the spirit. Tonight they were strangers sharing, by a quirk of fate, the same habitation and burning with resentment over it.

Joanna, hurt and bewildered, didn't know what to do about anything. Her desire was to come to terms with Simon at any price, but her pride asked did he want her to? She didn't relish being in this house with any woman out of his past no matter what the circumstances, yet as Simon's wife she could not escape the tenets of social behaviour and would be expected to play hostess, sympathiser, friend and sister female in all girls together sessions.

'Don't let it be for long, please!' she asked an unseen listener. 'I don't think I could bear it!'

Work was the anodyne during days that followed. Although there had been no terrible quarrel, withdrawal on both sides was complete. It was possible to meet and not commune at all. Words were spoken which were part of idle conversation, and silences allowed each to go about their own business. Two separate lives ran their courses during each day, and in the confluence of evening's meeting there was never any joining. Neither took the first steps to re-establish their former relationship. Joanna brooded that she was now an intruder in Simon's affairs; he privately thought that he had failed her, disappointed her hopes of this marriage and that she was wallowing in regret. He realised that something would have to be done about it. If she couldn't bear to live with him then he would have to release her, but patience must first be exercised. He would do nothing to offend her, least of all force her to bend to marital demands. It was unfortunate that she resented his gesture towards Katrina, and if the situation became really untenable then he wouldn't hesitate to ask the visitor to move elsewhere. When Kátrina had appealed to him she had thought of him as the perennial bachelor admirer, but what he had known of marriage had been Elysian and he could never return as happily to his old ways. He wondered secretly and fretted over what had changed his Joanna of the moonlight by the river into the moody, wary creature she now was. His invitation to Katrina had merely been added fuel, she had been burning before that, behaving strangely and thrusting him away.

Simon's work was of the curate's egg variety, good only in parts. He was having more than his fill of severed fingers, infected sores, industrial accidents, splinters in flesh and grit in eyes; these were the trivia of the house surgeon and could have been dealt with by any young fellow out of his internship. He was already missing the field of his speciality, though he did not care to admit it. At times he was a large fish out of water. He wanted to tell Joanna that she had been right in assuming that one tour of this nature would be enough, but he fancied she wouldn't be interested.

What serpent, he raged in his lonely bed, had entered his newly discovered Eden? Why didn't she come right out with it and say 'Simon, I'm sick of you,' or 'filled with revulsion from what we did together', or simply, 'We made a terrible mistake and there it is.' He hadn't intended allowing himself to care deeply for another woman, but this must be love which made hard labour out of breathing at times, which made an ache from his throat to his loins when he was alone with her and she looked so remote.

When the telegram came giving Katrina's estimated time of arrival he tried an approach.

'Joanna, Katrina MacDonald is coming tomorrow midday, by rail. I'll see that a car meets her at the station. If you like I can tell her you aren't very well and have her taken to the Imperial. I don't want you to be upset, honestly.'

She managed a smile.

'Simon, I won't have you telling white lies on my account. I'm perfectly well and Katrina stays here. In fact, I'll take an hour off and meet her myself, see her established and all that. I have no right to object and I'm ashamed of myself.'

'That's very nice of you, Joanna.'

'No, it isn't. It's merely good manners. I'm following your example. Your manners are always impeccable, Simon.'

'I—Joanna, there's one other thing. This is a small house. Katrina is bound to spot that we—er—don't——'

She helped him out. 'Simon, it's a very big bed and I don't lock my door. Katrina can't know what goes on inside the room. If you want to come in with me you're very welcome. Of course you can always explain that in this heat it's cooler sleeping apart, if you want to.'

'I don't think any normal newly married man would be much affected by the heat.'

She looked at him proudly, straight in the eye.

'Are you sure you want Katrina to think we're a normal couple?'

'But we are. Quite normal.'

'Oh, no, we're not,' was torn from her. 'We're a normal couple with a damned abnormal arrangement, and a pretty pickle we're managing to make of it!'

CHAPTER NINE

KATRINA MACDONALD settled in as the third member of the household very quickly. She was sweet and extremely grateful, profuse in her thanks.

'So marvellous of you to have me, Joanna, and practically still on your honeymoon, too! When I know my way around this town better I shall buy you a wedding present. I never thought the day would dawn when I'd be buying my dear Simon a wedding present. You were a sly old dog, weren't you? Not a hint in your letters. I do believe it was love at first sight when you met Joanna, and no wonder! But don't forget, my girl,' this with a playful frown and perhaps not so playful green-dagger eyes, 'I did see him first.'

'I know,' Joanna smiled back, 'and I'm surprised you let him go.'

'So,' agreed Katrina, with a meaningful glance in Simon's direction, 'am I. I needed my head examining. Still, what's done . . .'

They all went about together for the first two weeks, when possible, and then Joanna had a couple of late evening house visits to do and Simon and Katrina were left to go out, or stay in, as they wished. After this she found she was too tired for much social life—maybe this was the way early pregnancy affected one—so she made excuses not to be included in their plans.

'Don't you mind me going out with Simon like this?' Katrina asked her one evening, her eyes wicked. 'After all, I'm not exactly a hag, and we were once in love.'

'I'm the trusting type,' Joanna said with a tight smile. She was, by now, more than a little sickened by Katrina and her innuendoes.

'I think that's an extremely dangerous admission and a challenge to any red-blooded woman. Why don't you come with us, Joanna, like you used to?'

'Because I'm too tired after a long day's work, Katrina, but I don't object to Simon going out in the least.'

'I think you're very clever. All the time he's out he's wondering about you and worrying about you. You obviously know how to get him and play his weakness.'

'Simon weak?' Joanna laughed. 'He's impregnable.'

'I wouldn't say that, Joanna,' Simon demurred, coming forward and fiddling with his bow-tie, a task which Katrina promptly took upon herself, reaching up on her toes and leaning against him, which left Mrs Rivers feeling slightly sick. 'I have my vulnerable places, but naturally don't wish to reveal them. Look what happened to Achilles.'

Katrina was looking breathtakingly lovely in a sleeveless green dress and bolero jacket. Her dark red hair was piled high on her head and she was subtly made up with pale green eye-shadow bringing out the lights in her green eyes. She was naturally pale, as people with this colouring usually are, and her skin was waxen, obviously having always been protected in this blistering climate.

Simon hesitated as Katrina tripped off to the car.

'Are you sure you won't come, Joanna?'

'No. No, thanks.'

'It's best I take her out of the way if you're tired, isn't it? I mean you—don't mind?'

'I'm not a dog in the manger, Simon, or whatever one does call one of my sex in the same context.'

They both laughed and then looked constrained at their own laughter as though it had brought them too close for comfort.

'Well, goodnight, Joanna. I'll try not to wake you.'

But she was wide awake at midnight and they hadn't returned, still awake at one-fifteen when she heard

Katrina giggling rather tipsily and stumbling up the veranda steps. Katrina was certainly making no effort to be considerate of others, for she spoke querulously.

'Simon, I—feel funny.'

'Sssh!'

'Put me to bed. Kiss me goodnight.'

A further shushing and then a long period of complete silence. Joanna began to sweat into her pillow. Her hands were clenched and she felt as though a blood-pressure cuff banded her whole body. Eventually Simon crept into the room and disrobed in the dark. She felt him depress the mattress as he climed in on his side, but the bed was so wide they didn't touch. For a few moments her nose had been tickling and now she could control the sneeze no longer.

'Bless you!' came Simon's voice.

'What?'

'I said "Bless you"!'

'Oh, yes, I see. Thanks.'

'I'm afraid we disturbed you. Katrina is inclined to be rowdy in her cups. I had to gag her eventually.'

With your kisses, Joanna thought bitterly, and you had to assist her into her bed, as you once did me. Aloud she said, 'You didn't disturb me. I wasn't asleep properly.'

'Why are you sleeping so badly, Joanna? Do you usually suffer from insomnia?'

'No. The nights are so hot. But not to worry. I firmly believe we get all the sleep we need.'

'You're keeping well?'

'Fine, thanks.' This was true. The trouble each morning was now negligible and she took it in her stride. Her hair seemed more luxuriant and her eyes bright and large. She experienced moments of exultation and others of deep depression, but these phenomena of pregnancy interested her as her knowledge had previously come from books.

After three weeks Katrina was firmly entrenched in the household and did not suggest having plans other than to remain there. Other unattached European males began to date her and she was apparently in her element as the belle of Katsungi.

Joanna had gathered that Simon did not get on too well with his colleague Alec Bossom. For one thing Simon was the senior M.O. on the site and Bossom had been inclined to resent this fact from the start, thinking that seniority should be decided by length of service rather than qualifications. Also Bossom thought himself a bit of a ladies' man. He was fair, pink-skinned and had heavily muscled arms and legs. He had once come to dinner with the Rivers and made a pass at Joanna while Simon had been busy mixing drinks. She had removed his hand from where it was squeezing her knee and gone pointedly to sit somewhere else, regarding the visitor glacially thereafter. Now Bossom began to esquire Katrina, and Joanna could tell that Simon hated the fellow hanging about the house.

'I do hope Katrina doesn't make a dreadful mistake the second time too,' Simon said darkly one evening as Alec went off with Mrs MacDonald in search of the limited night-life of the town.

'What do you mean by "too"?' Joanna inquired.

'Her marriage to Howard MacDonald was a mistake. She was dreadfully unhappy.'

Joanna's voice sounded dry even in her own ears as she observed, 'Perhaps he was unhappy too. We don't know.'

There was a somewhat pregnant silence, then Simon coughed.

'You don't like Katrina, do you, Joanna? Oh, I know you're very polite and forbearing with her, but that's at the bottom of it. If you did like her you'd tell her off occasionally when she's using your home as a sort of waiting-room between dates. If I were in your shoes I'd have shown my true feelings before this. Why don't you tell her to meet Bossom at the Imperial for a change?'

'Oh, Simon, I'm surprised at you. If you're jealous of Alec Bossom, speak out for yourself.'

The chair which had been rocking on its two back legs fell with a crash as Simon rose. His incredible anger flamed in his countenance.

'What was that you said?' he demanded.

'I think you heard.' Her voice was uncertain, shaking.

He left her without another word and came back in half an hour under control, calm and very cool.

'Joanna, I want to make things clear between us. Say yea or nay to the following. One—you now think our marriage, an experiment in relationships, was a mistake?'

'Yes.' Joanna didn't raise her eyes.

'Two—you would like to be out of it?'

'If you would, yes.'

'Please don't consider me. I asked for your own reactions to the situation. You would like a separation? I think it can be arranged eventually. Answer yes or no.'

'I can't answer yes or no. I'm not being asked if I want beads for my birthday. I thought our arrangement could work and that for a while it did. But where people don't love each other there's always the danger that they'll want to turn elsewhere, and find they can't.'

'Is this a hypothetical situation or one which has actually arisen?'

'I—I think it's arisen.'

He looked at her long and searchingly. 'Oh, my God! I'm sorry, Joanna. I really am. We're both dreadfully unhappy as we are. That can be answered with a "yes", can't it?'

'Yes, Simon.' Her voice was a whisper.

'Don't worry, I'll think of something. I'm sorry I— rather lost my head on the ship. It complicates matters.'

'It was a mutual effort,' she assured him. 'That part of it was good.'

'But it's not enough without love, is it?'

'No. To me it's a part of love.'

'I understand, and I must say I admire you for speaking out, Joanna. We've more or less just divorced one another by consent and yet I find myself liking you. Do you object to being liked?'

'Not at all.' Her heart was a cold, cold stone in her chest and she felt she must die when this conversation was over, and yet she kept her chin up and determinedly faced what she felt to be the truth, out between them at last.

'There are bachelor quarters I can occupy on the site, Joanna. You don't have to put up with me so that you grow to hate the sight of me. I'll make some excuse as to why I only come here at weekends and then I'll sleep at the Imperial. Would you like to be shot of your job, go back home?'

'Don't rush me into everything Simon, please. The job's fine. Give them time to advertise for a replacement, at least. I could complete six months of my contract and profit by the experience.'

'What a terrible attitude! By the way, I think Katrina will be moving on in a couple of weeks. Can you continue to be forbearing a little longer?'

'I think so.' Here we are, she thought, discussing the end of the world, my world, that is, as casually as though we were discussing the weather. When it really hits me I would be better dead, but one doesn't die simply because it would make things easier. 'Is Katrina to be told we're parting?'

'Not at the moment. I can stall for quite a while if you can. If you're thinking of getting married I—I'll have to work something out with a lawyer.'

'I'm not thinking of getting married again, ever.'

'Oh. Joanna'—he sounded concerned—'you're not in love with some married man, are you?'

She began to laugh somewhat hysterically. Oh, Simon, you fool! she thought. I do believe you're nobly freeing *me*, but *I* can be noble too, if I try. She stopped laughing to admit bitterly, 'Yes, I am. Now, no more questions, please!'

'I'm sorry he's married,' Simon said quietly.

'So's he,' Joanna grimaced. 'But he may be free quite soon. Er—when will you be leaving?'

'Now. Right now. If anybody wants to know, there was an emergency at the site.'

She sat down feeling weak when the Jag had roared off, wondering why she had sent her unborn child's father away when, if only he had known of her condition, a sense of duty alone would have been sufficient to bind him to her for life. Who wanted duty as the cornerstone of a marriage, though? Katrina—his first love—had cried out in her need and his response had been immediate and typical. Now that Katrina was growing restive, seeing other men, he was uneasy, and it seemed clear to Joanna that he was regretting his marriage planned for convenience and longing for one that could be founded on love. Before there could be acidulation ending in bitterness, it was better that they should part and work out some sort of redemption.

Joanna had never thought much about divorce or imagined it could happen to her. It was something which happened to other people and she had always read of such things with a certain amount of distaste. She couldn't imagine Simon, the epitome of rectitude, doing anything immoral to procure a divorce, but she also felt that he would prefer not to live a marriage which had become a lie even though it was never ended officially in the courts. That was why she had told him she had no intention of marrying again so that he would not rush into doing anything to demean himself or his honour.

She worked so hard those following days that she became an automaton wound up but to serve one function, care for the health of sick humanity.

In a perverted way she enjoyed driving herself to and a little beyond her own limits. She came back to the bungalow exhausted and yet was driven to taking pills to help her to sleep. She ate like a bird and yet had more energy than ever before in her life. When thought threatened she picked up a medical textbook and rammed facts fiercely into her mind until there was no room for more, or she tackled yet another job which normally would have waited until tomorrow. She toured the squatter camp to visit her patients each evening; more families came in daily and dysentery was raging among them owing to the insanitary conditions they created. Government officials tried to disperse them, but they argued that there was nothing to go back to; crops had failed, livestock were dead and starvation stared them in the face. An American unit attached to the Red Cross set up soup kitchens so that everyone got at least one meal a day, and as this was more than they had been certain of for some time they became content to stay where they were, doing no work and sinking into the apathy which has always been rife among African tribes.

One day Joanna found herself acting as surgeon in the clinic. A small girl had been brought to her with all the signs and symptoms of an acute appendicitis, but over at the hospital several emergencies were already awaiting operation and they could not promise to take Malia until late afternoon.

'If you think she might perforate, Doctor, why not do the job yourself?' asked Doctor Hassan, the senior surgeon at the hospital. 'Your wee theatre is much better equipped than mine and I suppose the parents will want to take the child home anyway. I could lend you a student anaesthetist. He's quite sound, and an appendicectomy is so straightforward . . .?'

'Very well, Doctor.' Joanna wasted no more time in argument. It was some time since she had performed a major operation, but she remembered the procedure quite well, having done a couple of appendicectomies while acting as house surgeon to Mr Leonard back at St Paul's during her year's internship. She and Nurse Sabiya scrubbed up and were gowned and gloved; the instruments fresh from the steriliser were laid out under linen cloths, a crisp sterile sheet made the adjustable examination couch into an operating table.

Doctor Ajibo, black-skinned, white-toothed and friendly, came over from the hospital with all the impedimenta of anaesthesia and the operation was begun.

Joanna became interested in what she was doing. Why hadn't she opted for the surgical side? she wondered. The appendix, when reached, was swollen and inflamed, but had not ruptured into the peritoneum, and soon it reposed in a kidney dish and the closing-up routine began, then the stitching and finally an adhesive dressing was placed over the two-inch-long wound.

'We'll keep her until she's round,' Joanna announced, 'and then inject her with both penicillin and something to keep her quiet all night.'

It seemed odd, two hours later, to watch a child newly over an operation carried off on a litter by her family. Joanna told them she would call on them later that evening to ensure that all was still well. She told Siegfried to make them understand Malia must be starved for the next twenty-four hours, having only her lips touched with water.

Her ante-natal clinic had been delayed, but she now proceeded with this and it was quite dark when she had finished. Though she drove herself, her two assistants took it in turns to do overtime. This evening it was Nurse Sabiya's turn to accompany her on her visiting round and they called on two women lying in after giving birth. Both were doing very well, the babies thriving, and so on to the old who were dying and needed their shots of morphia for the night ahead. Next Joanna called on the young man who had lost his legs on the construction site. He was now fitted with artificial limbs, of which he was extremely proud, but his stumps were inclined to ulcerate easily and he was now on a course of streptomycin injections. Lastly Joanna was led to the shack where her newest patient, Malia, was living with her squatter parents, two brothers and baby sister. An old crone came across in the light from a cooking fire holding up her arms.

'She says we can't go in,' Nurse Sabiya explained. 'The child is being well cared for.'

'I'm going to see to that for myself,' Joanna said stubbornly. She pushed the sacking back from the doorway while the old woman made a peculiar wailing sound of dismay.

What Joanna saw horrified her. In the smelly little hut were seven people already; three round-eyed children sat watching intently, half afraid and yet fascinated; Malia's parents were drinking in the activities of an old, wizened, horrid-looking dwarf of a man dressed in a hyena skin and little else; he had necklaces of the teeth of many beasts and carried a wand topped by a grinning monkey's head which he was shaking around as though it spattered incense. But what was most horrible was that Malia lay on the floor in the light of a paraffin lamp, naked except for a grubby little apron covering her loins, and from her abdomen the adhesive dressing had been removed while in its place was a layer of foul-smelling mud apparently mixed with animal ordure. The child lay in a trance, or unconscious, while Joanna positively shrieked, 'What are you doing? What's going on here?'

The child stirred and whimpered, the parents looked uncertainly at the visitors.

'I'm sorry, Doctor,' said Nurse Sabiya, 'but this kind of thing does go on. This man is a witch-doctor and he has been asked to come and help cure the child.'

'Cure her? With *filth*?' Joanna almost spat. 'Tell him I'll have the police on to him. If he touches another patient of mine there'll be a great deal of trouble!'

The nurse interpreted, but Joanna noticed her voice was far too gentle, almost deferential. Even the enlightened did not wish to offend the old devils of Africa. It was akin to Europeans throwing salt over their shoulders.

Joanna felt no deference, however. In an unmistakable voice she pointed to the sack over the door and said, 'Get out!'

The monkey-headed stick pointed at her and a load of gibberish left the man's lips. Joanna snatched at the loathsome bauble and hurled it outside. The witch-doctor's eyes became dark pools of evil and he said something slowly and balefully before leaving the house.

Joanna was already kneeling beside Malia, cleaning the dirt from the wound and preparing another dressing.

'What did he say, Nurse?' she asked.

'Oh, nothing important, Doctor. Don't worry.'

'I'm not worrying. It sounded like a curse of some sort. I suppose he said I'd turn into a wart-hog or something?'

'Well, actually, he said you would never bear a child alive.'

A goose walked over Joanna's grave and she shivered before making light of the episode.

'The very idea! I hope you make these people understand that I'm very angry with them? This is my first meeting with the gentleman and I certainly hope it's my last. I shall tell the police about him tomorrow and hope he'll be removed for a long time to some escape-proof prison.'

'It's no good, Doctor,' the nurse said uneasily. 'When the police come inquiring nobody knows anything, denies having seen this man.'

'We saw him!' Joanna insisted.

'We saw a man visiting wearing animal skins. Lots of people do that to dance, make fun. Old customs are encouraged. We didn't actually see him doing anything, did we?'

'I don't think you want me to give information about this horrid little man, do you, Nurse? You're afraid of him.'

'One cured my bother's warts when all else had failed.'

'You too believe in him,' Joanna said incredulously. 'I suppose his medicine is better than mine?'

'I didn't say that, Doctor. I simply believe it's best not to antagonise such people.'

'You think I will never bear a live child, then?'
Nurse Sabiya looked down, but did not speak.
'I'll show you,' Joanna promised.

CHAPTER TEN

JOANNA burned fiercely with resentment as Alec Bossom arrived at the bungalow and promptly made himself at home. He said 'Hi!' and sat down at Simon's desk where he proceeded to borrow paper and pen and write a letter.

Joanna said sharply, 'Doctor Bossom, doesn't it ever occur to you to say "May I?" I sometimes think you live her and I'm merely your lodger.'

'Sorry, sweetheart. Don't mean to offend. I simply take it for granted that to a colleague this is liberty hall.'

'Well, I don't mean to be inhospitable, but sometimes you behave with what I call a cool cheek. That is Simon's private desk and contains private papers. Even I don't pry in there.'

'I'll bet you do on the quiet. No woman could resist.'

He rose and came over to her as she lolled against the veranda door sipping a bitter lemon. This was a Saturday afternoon. 'I'll bet you're not nearly so pi as you pretend, honey. You English women and your reserve are so much baloney.'

'I'm not particularly reserved with people I like.'

'Are you telling Alec you don't like him? Aw, come on! I'm a nice guy. You hurt my feelings saying things like that.'

'You can't expect everybody to like you. Frankly I find a little of you goes a long way. I wish you wouldn't come here so much.'

'I wonder! Being married to old Simon has told on you, baby. I'll bet he's still full of good English manners in bed. Or do you go to bed with him? Do I suspect a fracture in your marriage that he hangs around at the site with a delectable piece like you so near? I wouldn't leave you, honey. I'd be home like a shot and we'd——'

Her eyes blazed as he whispered what to her were insults.

'Doctor Bossom, I——'

He seized her and silenced her with a hard, fierce kiss. As she struggled he crushed until she was still and he kept her captive until she was drained of energy.

'How too sweet!' was Katrina's comment as she came up the veranda steps after a luncheon appointment at the nearby hotel. 'I suppose one must blame the climate, or something.'

'You don't think I was kissing him?' Joanna demanded as Alec merely grinned. 'I was being savaged.'

'I have heard,' Katrina proceeded succinctly, 'that it takes two to kiss. You weren't fighting very hard when I saw you.'

'Have we a date, honey?' Alec asked conversationally of the newcomer, as though nothing had happened. 'I see in my appointment book "See Kat at four o'clock".'

'You're not taking up with me where you left off with her,' Katrina said coldly. 'In any case, I'm leaving for Dar-es-Salaam tomorrow and Simon's giving me a farewell party at the Imperial this evening. You, Alex, are *not* invited. I'm sure Simon will be delighted to know that I found his wife in your arms.'

Joanna said, 'Doctor Bossom, please leave now. I'm sure you've caused enough mischief for one day. Don't come here again.'

'Well, and san fairy ann to you, my fine lady. You're not the only pretty fish in the sea, you know.'

Joanna followed Katrina to her bedroom where she had stalked in high dudgeon.

'May I come in?' she asked.

'It's your house,' the other said nastily. 'I don't suppose I can keep you out if you've set your mind on it. What do you want? I have to pack.'

'I'll help, if you like. I would be most grateful if you

wouldn't tell Simon what you saw a few minutes ago.'

'If you're as innocent as you say, what have you got to fear? Simon would probably knock Alec's head off or something, and that would be fun. I've never seen Simon doing violence.'

'I'd rather Simon wasn't told. It's not the sort of thing he would like to hear. Please don't tell him.'

Katrina's eyes narrowed.

'Answer me something, frankly, as a price for my silence, will you?'

'If I can.'

'Something's going on between you and Simon, and I don't mean the normal husband–wife stuff. In fact, I doubt very much you are a normal husband and wife. Simon dries up when I ask him and he seems to be very unhappy. Are you or are you not living together as man and wife?'

'No, we are not.'

'Why?'

'You said answer one question, and I've done so. Do you want my life history too?'

'No. I merely want to know if there's any hope for me and Simon. I have a right to know that, and he won't discuss it. He's a terribly moral person, and while he's tied to you he wouldn't. He won't even kiss me, though I try very hard to make him. You see, if I want something there are no holds barred, and I happen to want Simon. You don't want him, obviously, so don't be a dog in the manger.'

'I'm not being. We've agreed to separate. It—it didn't work out. Is that what you wanted to know?'

'Yes. Now I can really turn on the heat when he comes to Dar-es-Salaam.'

'Simon's visiting you there?' asked Joanna startled.

'He's taking me home tomorrow. He has a week off duty. Didn't you even know that? He's helping me get myself out of this damned country and back to England. One needs a man about the place to organise a move.'

Joanna felt weak with shock. Simon had been gone from the house for two weeks, but he had called in occasionally and they had shared a drink and amicable conversation, but he hadn't mentioned having a week's leave due to him or that he was planning a trip. She felt hurt and deceived.

All this day she had felt vaguely unwell and rather sick. Her head was raging and the contretemps with both Alec Bossom and Katrina had not improved matters. She suspected she was starting a malarial attack, especially when cramps in her middle almost made her double up.

Fortunately she was not expected at Katrina's farewell party. She had been asked, diffidently, but she had had more than enough of Mrs MacDonald and her polite refusal had been received with obvious relief.

After tea Joanna decided to retire to her bed. The pains were getting quite alarming and she was glad it was the weekend to give her a chance to get over the attack. By seven o'clock she was feeling so ill that she faced a fear she had so far kept secret. Could it be possible that she was facing the threat of a miscarriage? As a doctor she felt that she should know, but as a woman she was new to pregnancy and the rhythm of the muscular contractions were beginning to tell their own tale.

She rang the bell by her bedside. Richard appeared inquiringly.

'Madame sick?' he asked in concern.

'Yes, Richard, I need a doctor.'

'Master——'

'No, Richard, not Master. I want you to fetch Doctor Robinson from the hospital. Take your bike. Please hurry.'

Richard was back within fifteen minutes. Doctor Robinson had been called out to the scene of an accident. It wasn't known when he would be back.

Joanna began to panic a little. It seemed terribly important to preserve the life within her. There were that horrid old man's curse-words to belie, that she would never bear a live child. She must, for the sake of all her patients, prove he was phoney and fallible. With coincidental successes these people would continue to practise their dark arts, retarding the hand of progress wherever it threatened them.

She sent Richard to ask Mrs MacDonald to call in and see her. Katrina swept in looking beautiful in yellow satin.

'What is it?' she asked a little impatiently. 'I was just off. I believe my escort is waiting. Aren't you well?'

Joanna, looking deathly pale, found she couldn't confide in this woman.

'No. Would you please ask Simon to come home?'

'Oh, my dear, don't be a spoilsport.'

'Please ask him!' Joanna shouted. 'Surely you can spare him for ten minutes?'

'Oh, very well.' Katrina shrugged out of the room. A minute later a car roared away.

After an hour the boy, Richard, who was hovering near his mistress's bedroom, heard a low scream of animal pain and the sweat poured down his dusky countenance. He had been a houseboy for ten of his twenty-four years, mostly in the houses of Europeans, owing to his command of English, which the Mission fathers had taught him during the four years of his schooling. But Europeans, though they all looked alike to the lad, were vastly different in their treatment of him. He had been bullied, chastised, beaten to within an inch of his life for stealing a piece of soap and made to feel not only black but inferior and even dirty.

This madame, however, was always kind; not soft, let it be understood, but kind. She said, 'Don't steal the soap and cigarettes, Richard. If you want them, just ask.' She took an interest in his marital problems—he was saving up to buy a wonderful wife in a neighbouring town—and his madame had said she would ask the master to raise his wages and bank his money for him, to bring this desirable event nearer.

The lad didn't quite know what was wrong with his madame, but he felt in his heart that it was serious and that she might die. She had asked for a doctor and she was still in there alone and crying out. He had heard her tell the other madame—the bad one—to tell the master, and Master hadn't come. The telephone—that devil instrument—wasn't talking, so it was up to him, Richard, to do something more for his madame.

Richard changed out of his brass-buttoned white jacket and donned a clean shirt. He then took his bike, a shining new Raleigh with dynamo and hubcaps and a klaxon horn, and pedalled off furiously into the night.

Tundi Sabiya looked haughtily at her visitor when he hammered on the door of the small house she shared with her widowed mother and three sisters—she was preparing to go dancing at the 'Golden Slipper'—but when she heard that Doctor Rivers was ill she too was concerned and was out of her finery in less than five minutes. At the bungalow it took her even less time to see what was happening and her heart sank within her. Though she was still a prey to the superstitions of her country, and believed the witch-doctor's curses would come about unless he was propitiated and the curses withdrawn, she was still first and foremost a trained nurse and set to work making her patient as comfortable as possible. She opened the bedroom door to call to Richard, 'Find your master. Tell him to come here at once.'

Richard was almost turned out of the Imperial Hotel, the classiest place in Katsungi, in spite of his clean shirt, but he persisted and eventually saw his master at the bar, drinking alone in spite of many laughing people dancing and chattering in the ballroom beyond. He touched him deferentially on the arm and gave the message. 'Bwana, you come. Nurse Sabiya say quick. Madame much sick, very bad.'

Simon's eyebrows rose.

'My wife is sick?' he asked. 'How do you mean sick?'

'Bwana, I do not know. She sick, all I know. She tell Madame MacDonal' you come home. You no come. Now she too sick to ask.'

Simon looked over his shoulder to where Katrina was lying like a limp doll against a broad Canadian chest, slightly tipsy and oozing sex. Something like loathing dried up his throat so that it burned and his heart thudded with anxiety in his chest. He bundled the boy with him down the ornate staircase and out to the Jag which was parked by the open drainage ditch. They accomplished the journey in three minutes flat, running down a fat rat in the process.

Simon was in the house like a lightning streak, meeting Nurse Sabiya emerging from Joanna's bedroom with a stained pail in her hands.

'I'm very sorry, Doctor Rivers, but your wife has had a miscarriage. I think if she had been helped earlier it might have made all the difference. When I came it was too late.'

Simon looked beyond her to the pallid figure in the large bed, looking small and pinched and far away. The doctor in him made him take the pulse automatically and lift an eyelid for signs of life. Joanna was weak and bloodless and wanted only to be left alone now that pain was over. The husband in him hated himself for not knowing his own child had seeded in her, hated Katrina for not delivering the message which might have saved that tiny life, and felt weighed down with love and remorse that when

Joanna had cried out to him he had not been there to help her.

Four days and three blood transfusions later, Joanna watched a dark-skinned woman doctor remove the transfusion needle from her arm, in some relief. A square of Elastoplast was placed over the bruise made by the puncture and then the doctor smiled.

'You've a haem count of ninety-three now, Doctor Rivers, so I think you'll do.'

'So do I, Doctor Desai.' The woman came from Southern India and had trained in Madras. 'I'm feeling fine. A fraud lying here.

'Not at all. We'll have you sitting up in a chair today. Slowly, slowly—you know?'

'I know,' Joanna sighed, 'but I hate it. I want to get back to work.'

'No need to rush. Locums are employed to fill in where they are needed and your clinic is being manned—or rather, womanned—by Doctor Elsie Froome. She's a Kenyan and very experienced. So don't worry.'

Joanna wasn't so much worried as jealous. She didn't like the idea of any locum taking over her job, sitting in her chair and visiting her patients. For two days after her illness had reached its sad conclusion she had been barely aware of her surroundings, only waking from an endlessness of sleep to gaze dazedly at the white walls of a spruce little room with muslin curtains stirring in the draught from an overhead fan and flowers—a bank of flowers—completely lining one wall. The third day she was a little better and was told she was in the St Agnes' Nursing Home for Women in a town called Arusha, seventy miles from Katsungi.

It was really a maternity home, where white residents came to have their babies, but Joanna's less happy event put her even more in need of the expert knowledge which was now bestowed on her. The Director of the Nursing Home, Doctor Smithson, a

Rhodesian, had been in that morning to chat with her reassuringly.

'We found a malarial parasite in your blood, Doctor, and that would cause a miscarriage without the injection of necessary antibodies. If only you'd come to me when you first knew. . . .'

'I know now, Doctor. I was so busy and so excited, not even one hundred per cent sure, and I just didn't think.'

'But don't think it has to happen again. You've probably developed antibodies now. No reason why you shouldn't have a family. . . .'

Behind Joanna's smile remembrance was hammering the words, 'never bear a child alive', and her heart was sick with fear and doubt, the doubt that a single trouble begets a herd of the same.

Just before tea-time she was helped out of bed and into her dressing-gown. Her legs felt peculiar and folded up like jack-knives as she sank into an easy-chair by the window overlooking a garden glorious with hibiscus and poinsettias, cannas and agapanthus lilies as blue as a summer sky. She took a mirror out of her bag and viewed her brown eyes in their purple-bruised sockets. Her cheeks were still dead white, like paper, and her hair hung loose, making her look absurdly young.

'What a hag!' was her typical comment as she put the mirror away. Fortunately she was feeling very much better than she looked.

A nurse came in, plump and black and shining with a gash of a smile like snow. She wore a blue print dress and a dark belt. Pulling an adjustable table across Joanna's knees, she said, 'Tea for two, Doctor, then back to bed.' She set out two cups and saucers, two plates, a dish of sandwiches and another of cakes. 'Your visitor will bring the tea in,' she smiled again, and made her exit.

Tea for two—visitor? Maybe the padre who had been so kind, visiting her night and morning since her arrival here. Or maybe——?

The door opened and Simon stood there, very tall and incongruous with a tray of tea in one hand and a spray of white roses in the other. Joanna closed her eyes and told herself she hadn't really been hoping. Of course they had told her, when she was so ill, that Simon had been in and out like a ghost, dashing back to Katsungi to get her locum organised and then back again to Arusha, to and fro down a red-dust inferno of a pot-holed road several times a day. Then, yesterday, when she had been sleeping deeply and naturally, recovering, he wouldn't disturb her. He had peeped in and gone away and she hadn't been aware of him.

He tossed the roses behind him and set down the tray.

'Well,' he said, 'this is better. How are you feeling?'

'Fine, thank you.' She knew he must have inquired of her doctors before seeing her and would know the medical facts. 'I'm afraid I—made a mess of it.'

He would know what she meant, though they had never discussed the subject of her condition together.

'I wouldn't say that. Of course I wish I had known.'

'I'm sorry.' She began to pour the tea, feeling suddenly constrained. 'I didn't want you to think you had to stand by me, anything like that.'

He said, 'Don't you think *he* would have wanted me to stand by him—our son? It would have been a boy, you know.'

'No, I didn't know.' A hand had suddenly squeezed at her heart making her feel strangely bereft. 'Still, as it happens, the question doesn't arise any more. You have two sugars in tea, don't you, Simon?'

Simon said, setting down his cup. 'I'm back at the bungalow, you know.'

'Oh.' Her voice was expressionless. 'I'm sorry you missed your trip. Perhaps it isn't too late. I'm getting on very well and you needn't worry about me any longer.'

'Thanks. Which trip had you in mind?'

'To Dar-es-Salaam to help Katrina get away. As she says, one needs a man to organise a move like that.'

Simon's expression was politely interested.

'If Katrina needs a man she'll get one. It doesn't have to be me, and I have no intention of going to Dar-es-Salaam.'

'Oh, I see.'

'I don't, frankly. I suppose Katrina told you it was all cut and dried? She knew I had a week's local leave and no doubt presumed I was hers to command. Well, she's there, I'm here, and I'm not fretting.'

'Don't you like Katrina any more?'

'I haven't "liked" Katrina for years in the sense that I wouldn't trust her with my confidence. I was sorry for her in her trouble until I discovered she wasn't really troubled herself. She had grown tired of Howard and fate played right into her hands. You haven't been thinking that I . . .?'

'I'm sorry. I think she still likes you. She said so.'

'Katrina tells *my* wife that she still likes *me*? How typical! I wish you'd pulled her hair out by the roots or something. But let's discuss factual situations. Your preferences for company other than mine. Without bitterness, Joanna, I don't know who he is. I'm sure he would want to visit you.'

'No, that's all right.'

'Forgive me, but it wouldn't be—Bossom?'

'No, it wouldn't,' Joanna flashed at him. 'I suppose Katrina put that idea into your head too?'

'Well——'

'She caught that devil practically assaulting me in my own house. She suggested you might like to knock his head off. Well, go ahead. I wish you would.'

With his tongue in his cheek Simon said, 'You wouldn't have thought up this other man with the idea of making me feel better about my supposed passion for Katrina, would you?'

Their eyes met uneasily and Joanna's glimmered suddenly. 'There isn't another man in Katsungi I've even noticed, Simon. You are rather distinguished, you know. Nobody else can hold a candle to you.'

'Have we been—foolish, Joanna?'

'I think we have. The trouble is that because of our original arrangement we don't really feel we belong. I relinquished you, when I fancied you wanted to go, rather too readily.'

'And I was too touchy by far. Of course, if I'd known you were pregnant I'd have put it down to foolish whim. That would have explained a lot.'

'Simon, what are we going to do?'

'We're going to be a lot older and wiser, I think. I have no intention of giving you grounds for divorce. If you don't want me you'll have to lock me out and send me warnings of intent in triplicate. I shan't believe you otherwise.'

'I can't see myself doing that. I—I've missed you, Simon.'

That was enough. The china fell to the carpet as he seized her in his arms to drink those sweet words from her lips.

'Joanna! Joanna! How could you think . . .? You're all I want of integrity and sincerity in a woman, not that travesty of faithfulness we housed while she shopped around among the men in our district. I was ashamed of her, not jealous. I've known *you*. I crave no other woman. In a couple of years there's no reason why we shouldn't have a child. Smithson says so.'

Joanna leaned back to say, 'In a couple of years? That's a long time. I want——'

'No, love, don't let's rush things. You have to get strong and there must be no risk. Back in England I'll put you in the best hands.'

Though she was so happy Joanna's heart sank a

little. It was so important to her to produce a live child here in Katsungi, but Simon would scoff if she told him about the witch-doctor and his curse. Already she believed a little in the curse, because of what had happened, and she wanted to shed this wicked and horrid belief as soon as possible.

It was a month before Joanna returned to work, a very happy month on the whole, for she soon felt her old self again and the threat of Katrina had been removed for ever from the marital scene. She and Simon came together again in every sense of the word, quite naturally and ecstatically. They were good companions, joyous mates. The only cloud in Joanna's sky during those early weeks of reunion was Simon's adamance in insisting that her maternal instincts be suppressed for the time being.

This was not easy when those very instincts had recently been aroused by nature and then so bitterly denied. The scrap that Simon said would have been a son, though it had never breathed, now had a pathetic identity for her. She would sigh to herself, 'Oh, my poor little Johnny!' and in her sleep her arms would bend themselves into a cradle and sometimes she awoke with tears coursing down her cheeks.

Simon was not unaware of the emotional cataclysm which had taken place in his wife. His Joanna had so much to give and had kept herself bottled up for so long that the weight of her feelings had built up like steam pressure and needed to escape in periodic bursts. He, too, wanted her to have a child, but not again with risk, not again to end in the bitterness of disappointment. He was not so enamoured of this present adventure as he had been; he saw his colleagues' children with buff complexions, suffering their heat-rashes and malarias as did their parents, some of them had enlarged spleens from tropical diseases and none had the bright, bouncy resilience of all the London children he remembered in the streets back home. They played, but they quarrelled readily and soon became languid in the heat, cross and difficult. The average child here learned to whine before it could speak.

This, he determined, was not happening to any child of his. His children would be born in a temperate zone and run the gamut of complaints which could be overcome in childhood to build the strong foundations of the healthy adult.

Joanna tried argument; she was even inclined to harp on the subject.

'Supposing I can't have a child?' she threw at him one evening. 'Don't you see I want to *know*?'

He was very patient. 'Joanna, we've been married only five months, not five years, and I refuse to be hustled into this tremendous responsibility because of your hysterical fears. I'm quite happy just to have you at the moment. Of course I would like children eventually, but if they didn't come, well—there's adoption.'

'It's not quite the same, though.' Joanna screwed up her nose. 'That's a last resort. I simply want to try the first again.'

'No! No! No!' he told her. 'I refuse to use my sick wife as a brood mare. Now be content, Joanna.'

She looked up at him, hurt and anxious. 'Am I sick in that way, then, Simon? Did Doctor Smithson confide anything to you he didn't tell me?'

'No, he didn't. He said "in good time", Joanna, and you know as well as I do that doesn't mean next week or next month or maybe even next year. I was hoping'—his voice softened—'that I could make you happy, but I'm beginning to think, by your insistence, that all we have together is merely the preliminary for what you really desire; that it isn't enough.'

'Oh, Simon, you mustn't think that. I'm happier than I ever thought possible.' Now was the time to bring her secret, plaguing fear out into the open, but the very sanity of Simon's gaze upon her deterred her. She didn't want him to think she had given a moment's credence to something which belonged in the dark ages of man and his evolution.

'So can I come home in future assured that you won't bring up this vexed subject yet again, Joanna? Leave it to me to fix our child's birthday, my dear, as near as one can fix these things. Let all things be fortuitous for such an important event, and believe me, this place and this time isn't fortuitous. When you get back to work you'll forget this niggle to have that somehow you failed. I too want next time to be successful, for your sake as well as mine and the child's. Now, promise to shut up about it.'

'Oh, all right,' she grimaced at him. 'I promise. I must have been a terrible bore.'

'Never. My wife may infuriate, but life is never dull in her company. Now, when shall we ask the Petersens over to dinner?'

Lars and Ingrid Petersen were Swedes who had moved into the house next door while Joanna was in hospital. They had been very kind to Simon when they heard; Ingrid believed in doing her own cooking and many a dainty dish had found its way on to Simon's lonely table; he had also been invited several times to have his evening meal with them. They had three beautiful blonde children; twins Ilsa and George, aged six, and a baby girl of eighteen months called Hilde.

Joanna had spent much of her time, before returning to work, in enviously watching these living proofs of human love romping in their garden and occasionally in hers. Baby Hilde was an especial delight to see, blundering along on fat legs, falling down, picking herself up, or finding something so absorbing to hand, such as a handful of sandy dust, that she stayed where she was, busy and entranced. Soon she was crowing with delight every time she saw Simon, who was a natural favourite with all children.

This only served to make Joanna's heart the heavier at her loss. Her envy of Ingrid's family became tinged with resentment that one person could be so blessed and another—she hesitated to acknowledge the word—cursed. She was ashamed of such thoughts and told herself they were unworthy of Simon's wife even though Joanna Temple might have been capable of thinking such things. She tried to live them down by preparing a fabulous dinner for the Petersens to share; she went shopping and purchased red candles to decorate the table and made a sponge sandwich for Ingrid to take home for the children.

The evening was a great success and Simon was getting a bottle of brandy to serve with the coffee, as they sat on the veranda, when the Petersens' nanny, a really beautiful Tanzanian girl, came running in great excitement and distress.

She told the assembly that a cobra had crawled into the baby's cot and bitten her. While Lars and his wife stared in paralysed horror Joanna thought, 'I minded them having a beautiful and healthy baby, and now this! Maybe my resentful thoughts brought this about.'

She seized an unused fruit knife from a nearby table and leapt over the veranda rail, shoting, 'Tell Simon!' She was in the Petersens' house without realising how she had got there, tracing baby Hilde by her screams. The child was standing, clad only in a nappy, clutching the rails of her cot. There was a darkening swelling on her plump wrist and the forearm was also swollen. Joanna tied her handkerchief higher up the arm to stop the flow of blood and then paused only a moment, gazing into the wide, tearful questioning blue baby eyes before thrusting the sharp knife into the swelling of the bite. Hilde's cries were caught into an amazed gasp of pain beyond her infant comprehension as the dark, poisoned blood was sucked and spat out, sucked and spat out again.

Ingrid, from the doorway, cried out. 'My baby! She has cut my baby!' Lars caught her as she fell in a faint and Simon was on hand with a syringe of anti-venom to finish the job his wife had started.

'Well done!' he applauded her as the arm reduced to its normal size within a few minutes. 'That was quick thinking on your part.'

Joanna couldn't forget those round, horrified eyes regarding her as the knife had plunged, however. How could one explain to a baby that the knife-thrust was saving its life?

Lars Petersen afterwards apologised for his wife's exclamation. 'We are both full of thanks, Doctor. So full we cannot express.'

Baby Hilde could express, however. She screamed whenever she saw Joanna after that, a hideous, unreasonable, terrified screaming which would not be stilled. This went on for the fortnight before the Petersens moved house, saying the bungalow was a little too small for their growing family.

Simon caught Joanna crying furtively, a soft toy rabbit with which she had tried to appease little Hilde held in her hands. 'They threw this over the fence as they were going,' she sniffed. 'It seemed so unkind.'

'I know, my dear. I don't suppose they meant it to be. The baby wouldn't have the toy because it came from you, and I suppose the parents thought it would come in handy for someone else. Don't fret, Joanna. You're a doctor and are supposed to be semi-insensible. How many of our patients believe that even doctors weep? You name me one. When Hilde is old enough to understand they'll tell her about the other evening's shenanigans, and one day a beautiful Scandinavian blonde will seek you out to thank you. Mark my words.'

Joanna smiled with wet eyes.

'You always make me feel better, Simon. How true! Even doctors weep. But it always has to be in secret. In public one is not allowed to show one's hurt in case it interferes with one's efficiency. I'll miss the Petersens' blonde heads bobbing about, but it's just as well Hilde and I don't meet to give her a chance to forget her horrid experience.'

Joanna was relieved to go back to work and found her staff glad to see her. Apparently her locum had not been too popular and several clinics had been cut. Doctor Froome was not a believer in working after hours and had only seen the more seriously ill patients. Joanna, on the other hand, always believed in nipping trouble while it was still in the bud, so when the news circulated that she had returned to duty there were crowds of mothers dragging their children along for examination with minor aches and pains, loss of appetite and constipation. These were easily dealt with, but Joanna daren't dismiss anyone in case the apparently simple constipation was caused by an obstruction, the loss of appetite by leukaemia or some other fatal complication. She examined thoroughly and followed up where she was doubtful, and soon she was working through her lunch hour, taking only a sandwich and a cup of coffee.

She gloried in the activity of her new life, however, and appeared to thrive on it after her recent ordeal. She no longer wilted in the heat and discovered the secret of taking refreshing cat-naps of a few minutes' duration from which she emerged refreshed and recharged, like a human battery.

Simon thought she was looking lovely, and told her so. He also ached with love for her, but didn't tell her so, not yet wishing to impose his feelings on her if hers did not match his in ardour. He was now so sure of himself, though not quite sure if she had yet arrived or was still travelling joyfully. This not being quite sure one of the other kept them either side of a fine hairline in spirit, despite their physical intimacy. If Joanna could have heard Simon declare spontaneously, 'I love you,' her cup of joy would have run over; if Joanna had allowed Simon to guess at the depth of her regard for him, then this story might have ended now with the five words, 'They lived happily ever after.' But this is not a fairy story and Simon and Joanna were very real and extremely human people. They were too proud to allow their hearts to speak, and some breakers still lay ahead of them.

CHAPTER ELEVEN

JOANNA woke up one morning in January with the knowledge that she and Simon had now been a year in Tanzania; they had celebrated their first wedding anniversary two weeks ago with a *tête-à-tête* dinner at the Imperial during which Simon had presented his wife with an eternity ring, a hoop of platinum solid with tiny diamonds, and said, 'I really hope it is for eternity, Joanna. Thank you for this first memorable year.'

'And thank you, too, Simon.' She gave him her gift, a pair of onyx cuff-links. 'Even for the rows we had. It all made a wonderful whole. I'll try to—live up to you.'

'We may not see this tour out, you know. Our project is actually ahead of schedule and the ceremony of in-auguration is being planned for the first of September. After the thing's working, we hope, you and I may decide whether to stay on doing locum work up and down the country or claim premature end of contract. How do you feel?'

'I like my job, of course, and we've had some wonderful trips together—I'll never forget those few days at Victoria Falls—but I'll go along with you whatever you decide to do.'

'Well said, wife. At the moment I'll simply be glad to get away from Bossom. He's a troublemaker.'

'I thought all that had quietened down?'

'That's because I don't bring my troubles home, Joanna. He has always resented my authority, and he will do anything to belittle and rattle me. Also he sails too close to the wind in many ways and gets the rest of us a bad name with the nationals.'

'How do you mean?'

'Well, he goes with coloured girls. These people

have their own colour-bar, you know, and such behaviour causes bad feeling. The trouble with Bossom's
sort is that they come with the "Bwana" complex of
superiority and hand out their favours like largesse.
The rest of us are quickly tarred with the same brush.
Anyway, I didn't mean to bring Alec to my wedding
anniversary. I'm sorry.'

At the clinic things were now much easier. Most of
the agriculturists had gone back to their land and been
blessed with a successful season. They were being
gathered in the 'collective' system by degrees, one man
growing maize, another corn, another vegetables, yet
another tobacco, and all benefiting from the whole.
Science was accepted only slowly in Africa; it was hard
work getting shot of the old, time-wasting methods in
favour of the new.

On this day, also of anniversary, Joanna cracked
jokes with patients who had now become her friends.
One saw her for the first time, a boy blinded by trachoma who had responded to drugs so well that an operation had been performed which had now partially re-
stored the sight of one eye. He was awaiting special
spectacles and was very happy and lively as he came
from Doctor Webber's approving gaze to shake hands
with Joanna, acting as assistant at the opthalmic clinic,
as always.

The boy's name was Obajo, and a few days later he
was to loom largely in events at the clinic; dark
events.

Obajo was at this time sixteen years old and already
thinking the thoughts of a man. He was beginning to
show an interest in girls, one girl in particular, and his
recovering eye was constantly upon her so that she
consciously paraded for his delectation, pouting her
young bust and rolling her large eyes with all the in-
vitations of Eve. The girl's parents, however, had
other ideas for their daughter and these did not in-
clude the attentions of a widow's whelp who hadn't
any hope of raising the required bride-price for years,
if then. As their daughter grew more rebellious and

attracted by this forbidden admirer, even escaping from their surveillance to meet him on lonely bush paths, they decided to take further steps to dissuade Obajo's interest.

Joanna knew nothing of this story, only its consequences. On the day Obajo was to be fitted with his spectacles the lad did not arrive; instead his mother came to explain that his stomach had been sick for two days.

'I'll come along and see him,' Joanna promised. 'Probably a little gastric trouble,' she told Doctor Webber. 'I've made a note to visit him at his home.'

When she saw Obajo she couldn't credit the change in the lad in only one week. His mother told her that he had suddenly baulked at the sight of food. The very thought of eating made him feel sick and for three days nothing had entered his stomach, not even a drink of water. The recovered eye, which had lately been so bright and full of life, was now lack-lustre and he turned protestingly from the investigating ophthalmoscope. He had lost weight, but when she pressed into the abdomen there was no obvious enlargement of either liver or spleen and no tension over the appendix. The lad denied he had any pain whatsoever and his temperature was normal.

Joanna was puzzled. She advised the mother to feed the lad on soups, and waited while a little vegetable liquid was heated.

Immediately he smelled at the bowl Obajo vomited violently, however, and turned away to the wall, mutely indicating that he wanted only to be left alone.

'It can't be much,' Joanna said to the mother. 'Let him rest for a day or two and I'll call again if I'm needed.'

She heard nothing, however, and presumed Obajo was back to his normal health. His mother crept into the clinic one evening, four days later, saying that her son was dying.

Once more Joanna visited what had quickly become a living skeleton. Obajo was practically unrecognisable. He had had no food or drink for almost two weeks.

Joanna moved quickly. An ambulance conveyed the poor lad to the hospital where he was put on a drip-feed. All the hospital staff, as well as Joanna, examined him and subjected him to every conceivable test and X-ray. Doctor Hassan, the surgeon, spoke what was in his mind and was already dawning in others, though it came as a shock to Joanna.

'I think we've got another case of voodoo on our hands and may as well all go home.'

'You mean'—Joanna was aghast—'this is some sort of black magic in this day and age? You can't be serious!'

'I've seen it happen before,' said Doctor Robinson. 'We can't dismiss what we fail to comprehend, Doctor. My diagnosis will be death caused by malnutrition. The lad is starving to death.'

'But we're feeding him!' Joanna expostulated. 'We'll save him, in time.'

'We're trying,' said Doctor Hassan. 'We're scientists, but we're probably up against practices as old and experienced as time itself. I think somebody should try to find out what this laddie has done to offend and see if it can be called off.'

'I think it's ridiculous,' Joanna opined, 'but I'll certainly make inquiries.'

Joanna's inquiries proved fruitful and astounded her. She learned about the girl, Sereta, who had been unashamedly grieving for her young admirer, and so approached her parents, who didn't want to talk until the young doctor made some threats, one of these being that the husband would lose his job at the construction site if it became known he consorted with witch-doctors.

'It is the practice,' the man said defensively. 'The boy was after our daughter and we have plans to get her married to a rich merchant who will look after us, too.'

'So what did you do?'

'We asked a medicine-man to make a bad ju-ju to keep him away. We had already warned the boy.'

'Siegfried,' Joanna said to her companion on this occasion, 'you have just heard these people admit that they are helping to murder the boy Obajo? I will expect you to tell the police what you know.'

When Siegfried, who was a Moslem and not super-stitious, had interpreted this, the man and woman looked startled and protested furiously.

'What is this talk of murder? The boy was annoying us and wouldn't be told. What can parents do when they love their only daughter?'

'When they want to sell her to the highest bidder, you mean!' Joanna said angrily. This question of sell-ing girls—which was what the system amounted to—angered her, but she knew she was not there to criti-cise what had been common practice throughout black Africa. 'The boy, Obajo, is in the hospital dying from starvation. Whoever did this thing is a murderer, and I'll see there's a great deal of trouble for somebody unless something is done quickly!'

She could trust herself to say no more and went outside to gulp in fresh air and cleanse her thoughts. Of course she didn't believe, not even though this thing was happening before her eyes. If she allowed herself to believe, then her hopes of motherhood she must also believe doomed.

Hourly Obajo became weaker, despite the drip-feed fed into his veins. Next day he was in a coma and not expected to last more than a few hours.

In her clinic Joanna had a visitor who was not a patient. She was a very pretty young girl in a blue print dress with a yellow bandana tied around her stubble hair. She spoke enough English to make her-self understood without need of an interpreter.

'Obajo my friend,' she explained.

'Oh. Do you want to see him? He's in the hospital.'

'No, I not see him, I come tell you he be O.K. now. He get better quick.'

'I don't think you understand,' Joanna patiently

explained. 'Obajo is very seriously ill. He is not expected to live.'

'Oh, no.' The girl was adamant. 'He get better now. My father he have medicine-man make good ju-ju. Kill bad ju-ju. Obajo all better soon quick.'

The girl went off smiling happily and Joanna shrugged helplessly at Nurse Sabiya.

'I didn't seem to be on that young lady's wavelength. I couldn't get through to her.'

'Perhaps she merely intended getting through to you, Doctor. She was telling you that the wrong done to Obajo has been righted. He'll wear those new spectacles yet.'

Joanna stared, beginning to comprehend.

'Nurse Sabiya, you saw that boy an hour or so ago and he was sinking fast. He may be dead. Doctor Hassan promised to keep me informed. Now, supposing we get on with our work and forget all this mumbo-jumbo?'

An hour later a nurse came over from the hospital reporting a strengthening of the boy Obajo's pulse. During the next hour he came out of the coma and spoke to the nurse on duty, saying he was hungry. By six o'clock he was taking soup and smiling at the other patients in the ward. Two days later he was discharged as fit.

On that evening when the tide of Obajo's life had turned, Joanna went home in a state of panic and confusion. This was something she simply had to discuss with Simon and she introduced the subject over dinner.

'Simon, do you believe in this voodoo, ju-ju or whatever they call it?'

'I haven't thought much about it, my dear. They do say there are more things in heaven and earth—you know?'

'But this is neither of heaven nor earth. It's straight from the devil, if you believe in one of those. It—it's horrible. I don't like it.'

He regarded her closely. She was actually trembling as she spoke.

'Joanna, what's happened to upset you? This isn't like you at all. You haven't secretly become a member of a coven of witches, have you?'

'Simon this isn't a joke. I had a patient who became ill. No symptoms apart from nausea at the sight or smell of food. He was brought into the hospital yesterday, and you know what they're like when they're admitted to that place! He was a skeleton, just desiccating into nothingness, and there was a general discussion as to what was to go on the death certificate. You see nothing could be found wrong with him and he at no time ran a temperature. Then he began to improve and I left him sitting up and taking nourishment. He was dying this morning.'

'Well, who knows at what point the tide of life turns in any human being?' Simon asked. 'Everybody has a survival point and some can reach depths unplumbed by others and still recover.'

'You haven't heard the whole story,' Joanna proceeded. 'It appears that unknown to the lad he had had a curse put on him to turn his stomach from taking food. Today a girl came to the clinic telling me, quite blithely, that the curse had been lifted and all would be well. I told her it was a bit late for anybody to repent at that stage as all was practically up with the lad, but I was in for a shock, pleasant though it was. At that very moment the patient was opening his eyes and taking an interest in living again. I'm told by the hospital staff that this sort of happening isn't unique. Though curses concerning human life are illegal there's still a considerable black market in them. I'm extremely shaken and disturbed, Simon. I don't know what to think.'

'Obviously there's something in it, Joanna,' he said uneasily.

She rounded on him. 'What do you mean by something? I think it's awful that someone should practise dark arts like these. I want to believe there's an explanation satisfying to someone like me. I—I just can't believe in curses. Or, to be honest, I don't want to.'

'I think the African is influenced more than we are by the forces of evil in which he believes. The African has been taught to propitiate demons and devils rather than to worship God. He has an extra-sensory perception of evil. His subconscious is probably easily reached by those who have trained themselves to communicate through this medium. This is only my opinion, not gospel. I should imagine that whereas our psychiatrists get through to mentally disturbed people in the privacy of the consulting-room, here on this continent, people have known how to communicate with the mind for centuries. It's something which will recede as science takes over. You mustn't worry about it.'

'Of course I must worry about it,' she suddenly snapped at him. 'I saw one of my patients practically wished to death because he was looking at somebody's daughter in a normal, healthy way, and only saved because I went around dropping hints about repercussions if he did die. This power, if it does exist, is in the wrong hands and if it can undo all our good work, then it's a terrible thing and it—it scares me.'

'Joanna, calm down!' Simon advised. 'You can't wage a crusade against superstition and witchcraft on your own. I'm sure the authorities know it goes on and that they'll crush it out of existence eventually, but for you to go all to pieces because of one inexplicable experience is ridiculous. Anybody would think——'

Her face was livid as she waited for him to proceed, but he did not understand her mood and the words died in mid-air.

'Yes, what *would* anybody think? That I was a little touched? Suffering from bats in the belfry? I'm not surprised if I am, though you would probably retain your sanity in any eventuality. Well, today wasn't just Obajo, it was me, your wife. You see I got myself cursed by one of these charming gentlemen who practise the dark arts. Oh, I'll live. It wasn't a death curse; not for me, at any rate. It was a simple little thing

172

involving my offspring. They will all, according to the witch-doctor, be stillborn, and as I was pregnant at the time, and you now know what happened, you may be able, with a struggle, to imagine my state of mind after what I've witnessed today!'

Far into the night Simon tried to reason with his wife.

'Joanna, it was coincidence. You're not on their wavelength. Only being scared can harm you, unbalance you. You've got to forget this stupid idea that you're cursed. Now are you going to be sensible?'

'Simon,' she was snuggling close to him, 'I don't really believe in this curse in my heart of hearts, but don't you see? other people do. Nurse Sabiya really thinks I lost my baby because of it. She's half of our world and still half of hers. There are many like her who understand a lot about medical science, but would still go secretly to a medicine-man to have an incantation chanted over them if they were ill or troubled. I want to prove that these people are not infallible, because I think their power is more evil than good, and I can only do that in my own way.'

'What is it you want to do, Joanna?'

'Simon, please don't be angry. I simply have to go ahead with your approval and produce a beautiful, living, breathing baby.'

He was silent for a few moments and then his voice came soberly out of the darkness.

'Was this on your mind when you were so insistent that other time?'

'Yes. It's always nagging at the back of my mind. When the Petersens lived next door it was practically an obsession with me. The more time goes by the more I wonder and fear. Sometimes I think about seeking out that horrid little dwarf and having the curse called off, but that would be to acknowledge that it really exists and the me I respect won't do that. The me I respect would never know another day's peace of mind if it surrendered to an evil thing.'

'Oh, Joanna, I think I understand. You should have

shared this thing with me earlier. How many more secrets are you keeping from me?'

'None. I don't know why I bother, because I feel so much better when I take you into my confidence. But, Simon'—her hand caressed his strong, bare shoulder, reached up to his lips—'you will help me prove them all wrong, won't you?'

He caught the wandering hand with its thrilling touch, kissed it and imprisoned it; she felt the approach of his lips and turned her head expectantly.

'My dear, sweet wife,' he whispered huskily, 'it will be a pleasure.'

There were anxious days when Joanna knew once again that she was pregnant, and poignantly happy ones, too. This time Simon knew from the first and he could scarcely bear to tear himself away from her each morning; life was one long prayer that nothing would go amiss. From the start Joanna was under Doctor Smithson's expert care. He was inclined to say naughty, and well done, all in the same breath, but his eyes twinkled and he was obviously delighted. Joanna had decided to tell him all about her contretemps with the witch-doctor, in a lighthearted way, hoping to hear him say, 'Bunkum!' or something equally reassuring. Instead, however, his brow had creased.

'There's no medical evidence to prove these fellows have any physical power over a person's health,' he had said at last, 'but there's a heck of lot of circumstantial evidence which shows the subject isn't all baloney. The main safeguard is a mental barricade against them, which I'm sure you've got, that the old portcullis is down and all clear for an eventual happy birthday.'

Joanna was certain her mental defences were all that were to be desired, but nine months was such a long time to maintain them. Still, she refused to weaken, and she had Simon with all his physical and mental strength behind her and his pride in what he insisted on regarding as her achievement when it was really only a normal consequence of married life. She wasn't only Joanna on her own these days, she was half a unit of which Simon was the other half, and they were drawn even closer by the most blessed of events.

This was her last day at the clinic and she was guiding her successor through the routine. She had resigned, at Simon's insistence, as soon as her pregnancy had been confirmed, but three and a half months had passed before a relief would be found and make the necessary arrangements to leave her old job and take on a new one. Actually the dangerous period for a miscarry was almost safely over, and Joanna had worked like a beaver the whole time. Now Doctor Mai Jones was feeling much as Joanna had done as she had prepared to take over from Doctor Somers seventeen months previously.

'I know I shall never get everything done in one day,' her sing-song Welsh voice complained. 'When I planned to come out here I imagined something like a desert oasis with a few handsome chieftains careering about on horseback, not a dirty little town with most of my patients living in shanties.'

'Still,' Joanna comforted, 'you'll find the experience rewarding. A girl like you must be thinking of getting married one day, and the number of unattached males out here is unbelievable.'

Doctor Mai's grey eyes, behind their round spectacles, looked suddenly interested. She was twenty-four and had never had a serious boy-friend.

'Healthy, husky Canadians,' Joanna went on, realising the subject was of absorbing interest to the other, 'which is really better than all these mounted chieftain types for a clever girl like you. You must come and have dinner with us some evening and we'll ask a handsome engineer or two along.'

It was very pleasant playing at matchmaker when one was happily married oneself, Joanna decided. Playing was really all she had to do from now on, for in the house the boys did everything. If she blew at imaginary dust, Richard was promptly on hand with a duster and if she tried to move a chair to a new position he would say, 'Where does Madame want chair?' Once when she was poking desultorily in the garden, the garden boy appeared and asked for instructions. Maussa and Small-Boy were king and lackey in the kitchen. 'I can't find anything they'll allow me to do!' Joanna complained after a week of this.

'Take regular, unhurried walks,' Simon advised, 'and take advantage of resting and relaxing. You've been working so hard you're still as taut as a spring.'

So far Joanna had told nobody else about her pregnancy. She wrote her mother and one or two chosen friends regularly, but kept the great news still a secret from them.

'It's because I'm unsure of it coming to a successful conclusion,' she told herself one day when she was feeling a bit depressed. 'My portcullis isn't down as tight as it should be. Oh, why do we women have to wait so long!'

One of her regular visitors was Tundi Sabiya, who did know the true reason for Doctor Rivers' resignation from the clinic. She was most eager to hear of her progress.

'Oh, I'm fine,' Joanna assured her, just as regularly. 'Doctor Smithson says everything is progressing quite normally. Why, yesterday I felt it move for the first time. It was wonderful. I can't imagine what Victorian ladies found about the quickening that made them want to faint. I was thrilled to bits. So you see, Nurse, it *is* a living child. You must believe that.'

'Of course your baby is alive, Doctor,' Tundi said with a big gash of a smile, but her dark eyes were veiled and Joanna knew only her words were encouraging. Her mind was going over the substance of the curse, that this living child would never be born alive.

'I'm well on the way now,' Joanna insisted heartily. 'If we're back in England when my child is born I'll send you a photograph by air-mail.'

'Oh, so you may return to U.K. before the birth?'

'My husband will be finished at the site in two more months and he doesn't want to take another appointment. Why? Did you want to be a godmother? That can still be arranged, by proxy.'

'That would be an honour, of course. I rather hoped I would be allowed assist at this birth. But if you're not here . . .'

'What you mean, Tundi, is that you want to throw off the shackles of superstitition from your own shoulders. You want me to prove that witch-doctor wrong, don't you?'

'If you did, Doctor Rivers, then I would boast about it among my people and it would spread a great deal of reassurance and good. You may think my interest is inclined to be obsessional, but I once had a sweetheart who went off his head after being warned that he would do so if he continued to take a certain course of action. His mother had died in an asylum for the insane and I'm not sure how much Cheddi was affected by the curse and how much by heredity. I don't want to live in this fear, so I look to you.'

'Tundi,' Joanna said sincerely, 'even if I have to send you your air fare to London you shall hold my living child in your arms at the christening. Now stop worrying.'

She wished she felt as supremely confident after her visitor had gone, but just then a sharp movement in her middle brought her up short and made her smile indulgently.

'Go ahead, little darling,' she crooned softly. 'I simply can't wait to see what you'll be like, but it doesn't really matter so long as you're fit and happy.'

The days passed pleasantly enough when Joanna succeeded in smothering that dark doubt in her mind; the rainy season came and passed, leaving the bush bright with blossoms of flame of the forest and tulip trees, even the jacarandas donned their unbelievable blue and within a week had surrendered the flowery trumpets to the mud. It was like having glimpsed the bowl of heaven itself and lost it again. At the end of August the sun sailed untroubled through the sky and the earth hardened into cement—and dust—once again. Katsungi was undergoing a much-needed springclean pending the arrival of the Prime Minister, who was to undertake the inaugural ceremony which would put the newest hydro-electrical scheme into operation and bring prosperity, it was hoped, to the region. All buildings fronting the processional route received a new coat of paint and Joanna took a fresh interest in her walks, watching the ceremonial arches being erected and the fairy lights strung overhead. She was, by now, six and a half months pregnant, more confident than she had ever been, in excellent health with still quite a trim figure. Simon came home one evening convinced that she could take an item of news without allowing it to worry her.

'Well, Alec's been asking for it long enough and now he's got it.'

'The sack, you mean?'

'No, a curse. His present girl-friend is quite a belle, in a sepia way, and her father has tried without success to make Bossom give her up. Her answer was to move in with Alec and last evening the curse was put on him. He's to come to a bad end. Alec's laughing his head off. He says that was always a foregone conclusion and why not enjoy himself while he can! I don't think he'll lose any sleep over it.'

'I wonder how many of us are walking about with curses hanging over our heads? I think we should start a club or something. Not that I approve of Alec's method of admission. I don't believe in that sort of fraternisation. Anyway, come on and have a drink before dinner. We're having roast turkey this evening.'

They had just started on the delectable dish when an agitated African boy arrived at the back door. Richard took the message and came in to announce, 'Oh, Bwana, Madame—there has been a very bad accident.

Doctor Bossom is dead. You are required to certify death, Bwana.'

'How did it happen?' asked Simon, noting that his wife had grown suddenly pale and tense.

'Car overturn and fall in river, Bwana. When he pulled out—Doctor Bossom drowned.'

'I'll come.' Simon turned to Joanna, who was trembling with shock and fear. He hated himself for confiding in her, now. 'Look, Joanna, I have to go and do my job. There was no connection between the stupid curse and this, you know. Bossom was a suicidal car-driver, as anybody who has ever been his passenger will agree. We've got to keep a sense of proportion. I'll be back as soon as I can.'

It was a bad evening, though, for although neither she nor Simon had exactly liked Alec Bossom, sudden death is always difficult to accept when the deceased has been the epitome of life and living.

After a few days Joanna told herself that of course it was coincidence; Alec would have died so if he had not received a curse. Her child was living within her, she had proof of this every day, and it was up to her to keep herself occupied preparing for its birth and thinking absorbing thoughts of motherhood. She had to choose names, too, so that she and Simon could drop those references to 'IT', in capitals, which could so easily become a habit.

On the Great Day for Katsungi, Simon left early for the site. He was now on his own, but as many of the labourers had been paid off he could deal with the two hundred or so maintenance workers, who would hereafter manage with a first aid post manned by a medical orderly and a nurse. Today Simon had several auxiliaries in the uniform of the St John Ambulance Brigade. Temporary seating accommodation had been erected for fifteen hundred spectators, Joanna would be among them, and there would be the usual crop of faintings and falls with which semi-trained personnel could deal adequately.

The great dam gates which would provide the raw

materials for the power of the scheme would be opened by the Prime Minister officially, and unofficially by those qualified to control them. The dry concrete bowl of the reservoir would gradually fill and start the great dynamos generating. Simon said it would be a spectacle, and Joanna believed him. One of the engineers' wives was calling for her as Simon did not want her to drive alone until after their blessed event.

There was subdued excitement as the spectators' seats began to fill up. On the other side of the dam the paid-off labourers were perching like monkeys, wanting to see the fruits of their achievement before going back to their home villages or touring the country in search of other schemes which would employ them. There were rumours that the Prime Minister's motorcade had reached Katsungi town and then nothing happened, only the heat of the afternoon became overpowering and the white watchers wilted visibly in their places.

'Are you all right, Joanna?' Simon came to ask, handing her and Mrs Stephens cold-clouded bottles of Coca-Cola.

'Yes, thanks,' and 'Bless you!' the women responded, and Joanna watched Simon go back to his place of surveillance, tugging her heart-strings with him.

'He's so handsome,' sighed Dee-dee Stephens. 'I hope you know how lucky you are, having this baby and all. We've waited five years and nothing doing.'

'I am lucky,' Joanna agreed, 'and I hope you'll have a baby soon, Dee-dee.'

The excitement was almost too much when the motorcade finally arrived. All the engineers and officials were presented, including Simon, and then there were speeches, but as the broadcasting system had broken down only those near could hear what was said.

'Let's have something to look at!' Dee-dee pleaded, and then shrieked as the first gushers of water poured into the reservoir. Somebody else shrieked as a dark-skinned doll—or so it appeared at this distance—hurtled from its perch and lay ominously supine in the path of the encroaching waters.

'Somebody's fallen in!' gasped Joanna, and stared in fascinated horror as she recognised Simon scrambling and slipping down the side of the great bowl to the rescue. He reached the man amid cheers and pulled him to safety, where he strapped his broken limbs and organised his haul up to the top before climbing up himself. All the while the water was pouring through the sluices and at that moment someone in control became a little too enthusiastic and opened the sluices wider, possibly having been given the all-clear too early.

Joanna heard herself scream as she saw Simon picked up by the jets and tossed like a cork in the whirlpools of waters, sucked under and spewed forth as though he was an inanimate thing.

'Oh, God!' Joanna was scrambling down trying to get to him and Dee-dee was behind her shouting, 'Stop that woman! Stop her, I say!'

In the midst of horror and terror Joanna felt the onset of another enemy, pain. 'Simon! Simon, I'm coming!' she called out, her voice drowned in the thunder of the waters, and then, blessedly, nature stepped in and robbed her of her senses.

CHAPTER TWELVE

THE next few hours Joanna Rivers remembers as a series of vivid impressions, like a modern painting, all colour and not much pattern. Her comfortable, happy world, which had been made up of waiting for something tremendous to happen, had now been transmogrified by the onset of the occurrences themselves; her terrible fear for Simon's safety had brought about the very thing she had worked and prayed all these months to prevent, and now her child was to be born prematurely and, most probably, as lifeless as the last.

Doctor Mai Jones, herself a spectator at the afternoon's events, had been called to the medical building on the site where Mrs Rivers had been taken in a state of shock. As Joanna regained consciousness she was greeted by the not so reassuring exclamation in a singsong voice, 'She's in labour, look you! I'm not going to be able to hold things back till Doctor Smithson gets here.'

This was addressed to Tundi Sabiya, who had donned her uniform and looked spruce and businesslike and ready for any action. Tundi indicated the bed where Joanna's eyes were open and asking an unspoken, agonised question.

'My—my husband?' she managed to gasp out at last.

'Safe, Doctor. Quite safe. Don't worry.'

Don't worry! they said. Don't worry! when one had seen with one's own eyes the threat of the end of one's world. Whatever was threatening now was bad, but it was not the mortal wound losing Simon would have been.

She became rigidly and gaspingly aware of pain that was not exactly pain; a tremendous, physical organic urging that one's mind suspended in space, a disembodied observer of the body's travail, and then it all died down and Doctor Jones was chiding, 'Now do try to hold back, Doctor Rivers, please. We're trying to get Doctor Smithson here, and this sort of thing isn't helping at all.'

Joanna said something very impatient and most un-ethical about Canute trying to hold back the waves being as much use, as Doctor Jones would find out when she was in labour herself, and not to talk such rot, and then her breath died in a gasp as the serpent coils once more gathered and squeezed, gathered and squeezed, and there was only this tremendous effort in the whole of the world and it was too big and getting bigger and then less, less into an exhausted relief.

'Simon!' Joanna exclaimed joyously, as his anxious dear face came into focus. His hair was still damp, but he was quite safe and well. 'I thought you were drowning! I wanted to save you.' She was weeping easily and clug in a kind of desperation.

'Darling Joanna!' he kissed her again and again. 'I do love you so much, my dearest. I do love you so terribly much. They couldn't have drowned me.' He smiled a little emotionally himself; she fancied even tears weren't far off.

'This might be a bad do again, Simon. It's very—early.'

'Never mind, love. Think of yourself. I need you. There's nothing in this curse business. This could have happned to anybody. It's happening to somebody all the time.'

'Still'—her eyes became wary once more—'here we go again!' she managed to say, and Simon was still there when it was over, smiling that encouraging, watery smile, and leaping up to greet Doctor Smithson as he came through the doorway.

Such hard work it was, Joanna pondered with pro-fessional interest at times, determining never to treat childbirth lightly again or dismiss it to her patients as 'only natural'. She was happy deep down, though, because her soul, meeting Simon's soul, outside of their bodies, for once, had cried out their love and need one of the other. Pride, up to now, had made them over-cautious to the point of being inarticulate. Never again. Love was not a State secret to be kept sealed up in archives; it was not a rich meat which sickened with over-indulgence. Love thrived on giving, multiplied the more that was taken away.

Things happened fast as Doctor Smithson and his head midwife took over. When there was blessed peace at last Joanna didn't even ask questions. The experts had done all that was possible and God had already, this day, rescued Simon from a watery grave. She was dumbly content to bow to God's will from now on. She had even slid into a relaxed sleep when Simon's voice spoke softly into her ear.

'Joanna darling, take our daughter. You can only have her for a minute.'

Joanna's eyes looked moistly amazed.

'Simon? A daughter? Is she——'

'She's very premature and tiny, love, but she *is* living. Don't hope too much, but you do see you've beaten that curse? You've borne a living child. Nurse Sabiya's over the moon. It may be a struggle, but Smithson says he's seen smaller babies than this pull through.'

At last Joanna looked at the little red creature in her arms, eyes tightly shut and mouth agape, too weak to voice the cry it was trying to make, but its living breath damp upon her cheek as she stooped to press her mother warmth against it.

'Oh, Simon, we never bargained for a daughter. Isn't she lovely?'

He looked with pitying love at the scrap which was, as yet, by no means lovely except to one pair of entranced eyes, and back to Joanna, who was somehow twice as lovely in his sight and brave and dear and enduring.

'She'll be the loveliest girl in the world, if she makes it,' he assured her.

Again those kaleidoscopic impressions coloured the hours. A message from the Prime Minister, now leaving Katsungi, congratulating Doctor and Mrs Rivers on the birth of a daughter and wishing all three well. Then the enclosing box of an ambulance, the windows darkened against the harshness of the light and the outline of the oxygen-tented premature baby's cot opposite, where life had scarcely been claimed and yet clung tenuously throughout the journey to the nursing home in Arusha.

'Every hour is one to us, Mrs Rivers,' said the midwife. 'If she'll feed, we'll manage.'

Long day, no definite news, and then Simon's visit, and, suddenly, worse news.

'What are we calling our wee scrap, Joanna? I don't think she'd appreciate your determined John Simon, somehow. . . .'

'I've thought and thought, but I'd like more time, darling. It's a big decision.'

'I know,' softly now, 'but there may not be much time left, love, and she has to have a name. The—the padre's here.'

'Oh.' Joanna's brown eyes flooded despite her preparedness for such an eventuality. 'Well, she is such a scrap, after all. I—I'm glad we had her, though.' They were in one another's arms, quietly sobbing together. How could such an unfinished jot of humanity, without finger nails and eyebrows, seem so important and so very dear? 'You choose a name, Simon. If she'd been a boy I would have had my way.'

'Well, her natal day was quite an event in one way and another, wasn't it? How about calling her after the Prime Minister? She is a sort of Tanzanian, isn't she? He's Julius, so she would be Julia.'

'Julia Rivers,' Joanna said. 'Yes, I like that. Give her a kiss from me, Simon, in—in case. . . .'

'I will,' and he was gone.

All that night the scrap of humanity held on to life, however, and was still faintly gasping in oxygen when she became forty-eight hours old. Simon became hollow-eyed from lack of sleep and still he had a daughter to worry and pray over. Every time he entered the nursing home he felt an unseen golden rein tugging him towards the cot where the tiny creature lay naked, except for a napkin, her doll-hands curled and her tiny doll-body so small it was pathetic.

Julia became four days old.

'I can't stand it,' Simon complained to his wife. 'She just lies there and it's a bird's heart beating, not a human child's. It can't go on.'

Joanna said, 'She's tougher than anybody thought, and maybe she knows how much we want her to stay.'

'Sweetheart,' he said sentimentally, 'thank you. No matter what happens, thank you for entering into that miserable contract with me. I could never have expected the wonder and fulfilment I now experience. I'm sure I don't deserve it.'

'Simon, when did you find out you really loved me? Was it when Julia became a fact?'

'No, oh, no. I discovered it one evening when I found my registrar sitting all forlorn in an autumn garden, soaked to the skin and very miserable. I told myself I was a fool, that you'd never be able to think of me in the same way, and I was so happy you even agreed to marry me. I had to watch myself, so as not to scare you off. I must have talked a lot of baloney on occasions.'

'I thought it was the wisdom of Solomon. You see, when I did begin to notice you, I realised I'd been emotionally blind until then. I, too, was so afraid of overstepping the mark.'

'You mean we were both in love all the while . . .'

'I only knew I was.'

'Oh, Joanna!' They hugged, kissed and laughed, kissed again. 'And you thought I'd come here to be with Katrina MacDonald!'

'She didn't exactly help me to think otherwise. You conjured up another man in my life. Remember?'

'We were such fools. I had no intention of giving you a divorce, you know. I'd have done anything. Talk is one thing, but action is quite another.'

When Julia Rivers was five days old, Simon again

felt that tugging at his heartstrings. The nurse stepped aside for him to see, and there lay the same little doll, quite unchanged, somehow grown waxen. As he gazed he witnessed metamorphosis, however. The head moved of its own accord, like an awkward ball, so that the face was upturned, and the features contorted into anger. The mouth gaped and even through the oxygen tent he could hear his own child's voice raised in protest, the wrists uncurled and thrashed about and the feet pushed each other on the stick-like legs. The whole was bright scarlet against the white of the napkin.

Simon looked at the nurse uncomprehendingly.

'She's hungry,' the girl said happily, reaching for the pipette and feed of brandy and milk. 'That's the second time today. We tried to phone you there was an improvement, but you had already left. I'll feed and change baby now, Doctor Rivers, if you'll excuse me.'

He went in a state of daze down the corridor, meeting Doctor Smithson on the way.

'You've heard, eh? She's going to be fine now. Just fine. I may want to keep her for another month or so, and your wife, who's dying to be a dutiful mother, will just have to forget it for this time. There'll be other children, no doubt. In a few days I would take Mrs Rivers off on holiday for a week or two, if I were you. You'll be amazed at the change in little Julia when you come back.'

All this Simon dutifully discussed with Joanna, still in a daze of relief and thankfulness.

'You need a holiday, too, Simon,' she said seriously. 'Can you be spared?'

'Yes. There's a locum at the site and I need only return to work out my notice. They have my resignation in writing. In a few months we'll be home.'

'We *are* home, Simon. Wherever we are, with our family, is home. It will soon be winter back in England. We must think of Julia.'

Simon couldn't stop thinking of his daughter, however. He took his wife off on a touring holiday and they saw many wonderful places and peoples, but each evening he sought a telephone to inquire of his offspring.

'I can see who's going to spoil her,' Joanna said happily, indulging him. 'Suddenly I'm not enough for you.'

'Oh, Joanna! You say that again and I'll beat you soundly as you deserve. Of course I shall spoil her, *and* Johnny, *and* the twins.'

'You've got it all worked out, I see.'

'We almost had two children while trying to show we loved each other. What will happen when we really try, I can't imagine!'

When they eventually collected Julia, after Doctor Smithson's expert care, she was no longer a peculiar and rather pathetic creature but a real baby, with black hair and blue eyes, pretty even at that age and quick to turn her parents into willing slaves.

It was for Julia that Simon arranged they go the long and leisurely way home; this meant they boarded a luxury liner in Mombasa and cruised round south and west Africa, arriving at Tilbury when the daffodils were nodding in the window-boxes and the windy air was clean and sharp in the lungs.

It was just over two years since they had left on the *Chieftain* from a nearby dock, uncertain both of themselves and the future. Now there were still some uncertainties. Simon did not know how easy it would be to pick up the threads of his speciality again, but the profession needed him as much as he needed his work, and there was bound to be the right niche somewhere. Joanna, too, was beginning to feel an urge to work again, providing it did not rob her of Julia's babyhood. She was thinking of applying to the education authorities for a schools' appointment, or a family-planning clinic. Of course, she might have trouble with Simon. . . .'

He caught her eyes as he turned from hailing a taxi and asked with a smile, 'A penny for them. Come on, now. You were miles away.'

'No, actually I was right here. Just looking ahead. It was all rather wonderful.'

She settled back in the taxi, looking at Simon with Julia, in her new woollies, in his arms, and gave a sigh of contentment. It was a very sure thing really, she pondered, though we managed to make a great mystery of it. When Simon said it would be all right I should have believed him. Here we are, having been halfway round the word, and everything's so all right I could sing. Anyway, why not?

She began to sing, there in the taxi, and Simon, unquestioning, joined in. The driver thought, they're either happy or high. Gawd love 'em. I do like a cheerful fare.

Doctor Nurse Romances

Don't miss
December's
other story of love and romance amid the pressure
and emotion of medical life.

ANGELS IN RED
by Lisa Cooper

Staff Nurse Margo Prince had been quite happy with
her career, and the brotherly attentions of Dr. Angus
Wheedon, until the arrival of Dr. Paul Laker. Why
should it all change now?

Order your copy today from your local paperback retailer.

Doctor Nurse Romances

and January's
stories of romantic relationships behind the scenes
of modern medical life are:

THE ICEBERG ROSE
by Sarah Franklin

Looking after the glamorous actress Romaine Hart
during her stay in a Swiss clinic seemed the ideal way
for Leane to regain confidence in her own nursing
ability. And so it might have been, but for Doctor
Adam Blake's constant interference. Why wouldn't
he leave her alone?

THE GEMEL RING
by Betty Neels

Charity disliked and despised Everard van Tijlen,
the eminent Dutch surgeon whose fees were so
outrageously expensive. Then she found herself working
with him — and her ideas began to change!

Order your copies today from your local paperback retailer

Doctor Nurse Romances

Have you enjoyed these recent titles in our
Doctor Nurse series?

DOCTORS IN CONFLICT
by Sonia Deane

It was love at first sight when Adam and Jessica met
in Amsterdam, and when he asked her to join his
practice in England it seemed like an invitation to
Paradise. But this Paradise, too, contained a serpent . . .

NURSE AT BARBAZON
(Summer at Barbazon)
by Kathryn Blair

Susan Day was asked to spend three months at a
Castelo in Portugal, as nurse-companion to a widowed
noblewoman. She was looking forward to her visit —
then she encountered the Castelo's imperious owner,
the Visconde Eduardo de Corte Ribeiro!

Order your copies today from your local paperback retailer